Why did he care if she was back in town?

She doesn't matter anymore. Hell, she never should have mattered.

So why did every nerve in his body feel taut? Why was his heart racing at the possibility of seeing her again?

Why was he standing up and slinging his jacket over his broad shoulders?

Cole had things to take care of. He didn't have time for an unscheduled trip back home. Nevertheless, he scooped his cell phone and the keys off his desk and set off for Yella.

All he needed was closure. Something about the way Maddie had left him six years ago—without even so much as a goodbye—still bothered him.

He had to know....Was she the bad girl the town claimed she was? Or the sweet, pure girl he'd fallen in love with?

He hoped to hell he wasn't fool enough to chase after a dream again.

Dear Reader,

I used to be an addict to the column "Can This Marriage Be Saved?" in *Ladies' Home Journal*.

When we fall in love, we make ourselves incredibly vulnerable to pain. So many of my friends and relatives have suffered through bad relationships and divorces and gone on to make new lives for themselves. I often wonder how many of those relationships could have been saved if the people involved hadn't been hurting too profoundly to try to work things out.

Do you believe in second chances in love when the wound you've suffered cuts to the marrow?

When Maddie Gray returns to Yella, Texas, the town that vilified her as a girl for her mother's sins, she never dreamed the passion she'd felt for Cole, the rich rancher who'd rejected her and their son, could flare stronger and hotter than ever. But it does.

Then Cole discovers they have a son and becomes determined to find a way to make their relationship work—for the sake of their child.

But Maddie, who grew up without love, has always wanted to be loved and treasured for herself alone. She isn't at all certain she can find that with Cole.

Ann Major

ANN MAJOR

HIS FOR THE TAKING

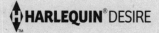

Recycling programs
for this product may
not exist in your area.

ISBN-13: 978-0-373-73248-7

HIS FOR THE TAKING

Copyright © 2013 by Ann Major

Printed in U.S.A.

HARLEQUIN®

www.Harlequin.com

Books by Ann Major

Harlequin Desire

Marriage at the Cowboy's Command #2101
Terms of Engagement #2131
His for the Taking #2235

Silhouette Desire

Midnight Fantasy #1304
Cowboy Fantasy #1375
A Cowboy & a Gentleman #1477
Shameless #1513
The Bride Tamer #1586
The Amalfi Bride #1784
Sold into Marriage #1832
Mistress for a Month #1869
*The Throw-Away Bride #1912
The Bride Hunter #1945
To Tame Her Tycoon Lover #1984
Ultimatum: Marriage #2041

Harlequin MIRA

The Girl with the Golden Spurs
The Girl with the Golden Gun
The Secret Lives of Doctors' Wives

*Golden Spurs

Other titles by this author available in ebook

ANN MAJOR

lives in Texas with her husband of many years and is the mother of three grown children. She has a master's degree from Texas A&M at Kingsville, Texas, and is a former English teacher. She is a founding board member of the Romance Writers of America and a frequent speaker at writers' groups.

Ann loves to write—she considers her ability to do so a gift. Her hobbies include hiking in the mountains, sailing, ocean kayaking, traveling and playing the piano. But most of all, she enjoys her family. Visit her website at www.annmajor.com.

To Ted

One

The last thing John Coleman had planned to do when he woke up to the stench of petroleum and the roar of his oil rig was to go chasing after Maddie Gray.

Jamming the phone against his ear, Cole—as everybody from Yella, Texas, called him—leaned back in his leather office chair and rubbed his throbbing temple. "What do you mean Maddie's come back to Yella and she's nursin' Miss Jennie?"

Miss Jennie had been their beloved high school English teacher.

Cole knew his soft drawl sounded mild, even disinterested, as he spoke to Adam, his older half brother, yet Cole was anything but calm.

During his marriage to Lizzie, which had ended when she'd died almost a year ago, he'd dreaded the thought of his childhood sweetheart coming back to town. Because he'd feared how he might react. But he was a widower now, and he'd been thinking about Maddie of late, thinking he might just drive to Austin and look her up. So far he'd always managed to talk himself out of it.

What kind of sap carries on a secret teenage affair with the town's bad girl and then can't move on after she treats him like dirt?

Hell, six long years had come and gone. And still his mind burned with memories of Maddie's fine-boned face, her heart-shaped lips, her violet eyes and ebony hair, and ample breasts. Why couldn't he forget how radiant her face had been every time she'd lain beneath him? Because she'd been more than beautiful. She'd been smart and gifted, especially with contrary horses.

But she had bad genes. Maddie's mother had stolen husbands, fathers—indeed any man who would have her. And in the end, her own daughter had turned the tables on her by stealing her boyfriend and running off with him, leaving Cole behind.

"Miss Jennie fell over a garden hose and cracked her pelvic bone," Adam said, interrupting Cole's thoughts. "Maddie's here to take care of her until Miss Jennie's niece from up in Canada can get down here. Nobody in town can stop talking about Maddie. About how well educated and classy she is now. About how's she's got herself a college degree and all. Cole, she's so damn beautiful she takes your breath away."

"You've seen her?"

His half brother hadn't moved to Yella until after their dad's death, which had occurred shortly after Maddie had run off, so Adam hadn't known Maddie when she and Cole had been together.

"I dropped by first thing this mornin'! All the guys have been stopping by Miss Jennie's place to check on her, so I figured I'd better check on her myself."

"Right."

"Just to make sure she's gettin' proper care and all. Oh, is Maddie ever beautiful. All curves and creamy skin. She has the softest voice and the sweetest smile—one that lights everything up."

"Enough!" Cole growled.

The brothers' telephone call had centered on ranch business until this last bit of local gossip. When Cole was away from Yella, Adam usually ended their calls about the family business by filling him in on the latest scuttlebutt.

"Well, don't you be going back there just to see Maddie, you hear." It was strange how much more annoyed than usual Cole suddenly was with his older brother. "You're to steer clear of Maddie Gray. I don't care how polished she is now, she's no good. Never was. And never will be."

"Something's sure got you riled this morning." There was an edge in Adam's voice now, too.

"Pressure here on the rig. You know how I was telling you this damn drought has shale frac water in short supply? Well, I'm facing the possibility of having to drill a deepwater well. All the drillers are overbooked except for one bandit who says he'll put me first, but only if I make it worth his time by paying him triple. And now you're distracting me with idle gossip about a no-good woman like Maddie."

"She's the interim CEO of some nonprofit in Austin called My Sister's House. She's worrying herself to death over some fundraiser she's in charge of in a couple of weeks. Sounds like she's trying to do some good, at least, doesn't it?"

"Camouflage! It's an ancient trick."

"Well, I liked her. Oh, and she's got a little boy she left back in Austin at camp. He's six years old. Noah. Miss Jennie's got loads of pictures of him. He's cuter than a bug. Black hair... green eyes. He reminds me of someone." There was an odd note in his brother's voice. "All in all, Maddie didn't seem the least bit bad. She's nothin' like her mother."

The last thing Cole wanted to hear was praise for Maddie, or her son. Especially not from his half brother, who often resented him because of their father's mistakes, so he told Adam he was a fool to fall for anything Maddie Gray said and ended the call.

So, Maddie was back, dazzling the town, even his brother. And she had a kid. Who was the father? Vernon? The timing would be about right. Cole had always been careful to protect her, so he knew the boy wasn't his.

Cole pushed his mug of strong black coffee aside so roughly, the steaming liquid sloshed onto several important drilling leases. With thoughts of Maddie stirring his blood, he didn't need more caffeine.

Edgily he shoved the papers aside and stared out the window. He slid his jean-clad legs onto the top of his desk and stacked one scuffed, black, ostrich-skinned cowboy boot on top of the other. It was early yet, but already a brilliant sun blasted the desolate Texas landscape. Thanks to his air conditioner, the interior of his trailer was icy. That was the only thing he liked about living at the drill site for weeks on end while he worked a field. But even the chilled air couldn't keep out the hot memories of Maddie.

Too well he recalled the first time he'd actually spoken to Maddie, who'd been younger and poorer than him, and hadn't run in his social circle.

He'd driven home from the University of Texas on a Friday and had gone looking for his girlfriend, Lizzie Collier, over at her daddy's ranch. It had been spring and the pastures had been filled with bluebonnets.

When Cole had stepped inside the barn and hollered for Lizzie, one of the horses, Wild Thing, had gone off like dynamite, neighing and kicking his stall door. Cole thought Wild Thing was too dangerous to fool with but Lizzie had the softest heart in the world. When she'd found out Old Man Green was starving Wild Thing and beating him, she'd talked her dad into buying the horse. Her father had hired more than a dozen horse whisperers to save the animal, and when they'd failed, Lizzie's father had wanted to put him down. Lizzie wouldn't hear of it.

Cole hadn't thought too much about the ruckus the horse was making until he heard a crooning voice inside the stall. Thinking Lizzie might be trapped, Cole had rushed toward the stall door.

"Lizzie?"

"Shh!" chided a young, defiant voice from inside the stall.

Since Cole couldn't see too clearly in the shadows, he took the slim figure wearing jeans and a baseball cap turned backward for the young male groom who worked for Lizzie's dad.

Fixating on Cole, the gelding's ears swept so far back against his narrow gray skull they all but vanished. Then the big animal lowered his head as his pale forelock shot over terrible eyes that rolled backward. Half rearing, the animal charged, his hooves splintering a board.

"Get out of that stall, boy!" Cole commanded.

Wild Thing's eyes rolled crazily. Again the gelding reared to his full height and heaved himself with murderous intent against the stable door.

The boy jumped back and flattened against the wall. "Are you trying to kill me?" In the confusion the kid's baseball cap hit the sawdust, and a lustrous mane of black hair tumbled down the imp's shoulders. And across *breasts*.

"Maddie Gray?"

What male with an ounce of testosterone wouldn't have recognized her sinfully gorgeous, exotic features—Maddie's creamy pale skin, her voluptuous mouth, her violet-blue eyes? Hell, she looked exactly like her no-good mother, Jesse Ray Gray, the town's most notorious slut.

Cole's gaze seared her ample breasts, which heaved against

her faded blue cotton work shirt. She'd filled out since he'd seen her last. If her tight clothes were any clue, she'd probably be up to her mother's tricks—if she wasn't already.

"You're Maddie Gray," he repeated accusingly, disliking her more than a little because she stirred him.

"So what if I am?" Her beautiful mouth tightened rebelliously.

Wild Thing's eyes rolled, and he neighed shrilly.

"Please lower your voice and start backing away," she ordered.

At least she wasn't a total simpleton. She saw the folly of being penned in such a small enclosure with a monster like Wild Thing.

"I said back away!" she repeated. "Can't you see you're scaring him?"

She began to speak to the startled horse in a sweet, soothing murmur Cole would have envied if he wasn't so furious at her for her foolhardiness and willingness to blame him for her own stupidity.

"It's okay, big baby. Nobody's going to hurt you," she said huskily in a purr that would have oozed sex had she been talking to a man.

A gray ear perked up. Not that the large animal didn't keep his other ear flat and a suspicious eye on Cole.

"You've gotta go," the girl urged when Wild Thing danced impatiently.

"Not until you get out of that stall," Cole said.

"I will, you big idiot—just as soon as you shut up and leave." For the horse's sake, she kept her insult soft and sweet.

Cole's stubbornness made him stand his ground a few seconds longer, but her pleading eyes finally convinced him. After Cole left, it took another minute or two before the horse settled and the girl was able to slip out. Strangely, no sooner was she safely outside the stall than Cole's temper flared again. He knew he should forget about her recklessness and go to the Collier house and wait for Lizzie, but Maddie had his blood up. So when he heard her light, retreating footsteps as she lit out the back to avoid him, he rushed after her. When she caught sight of him, she let out a cry of alarm.

Grabbing her arms, he shoved her against a wall. "You have no right to be on this property! Or to be in that monster's stall!" Cole yelled. "You scared the hell out of me!"

When Wild Thing screamed and sent his hooves crashing against wood again, Maddie stilled.

"I was just doing my job, okay?"

"Your job?"

"I'll have you know Liam Rodgers hired me."

Liam, Lizzie's daddy's foreman, was no man's fool. "Why you? Why would he hire you, of all people, when he could hire the best?"

She frowned. "Maybe because I know what I'm doing. While you've been off at college driving your fancy cars and chasing girls, I've been mucking stalls to get free riding lessons. Maybe I've learned stuff. When he saw Wild Thing stand calmly and let me saddle him in the round pen, Liam about fainted. When I rode the horse just as easy as you please, Liam hired me."

"Well, you can't possibly know enough to work with that monster."

"I did what twelve men couldn't do!"

"You got lucky! Now you listen to me. A normal horse weighs half a ton and has a brain the size of a tomato. Such an animal is wired to defend himself against predators, which includes humans, even half-pint girls like you."

"I know all that!"

"That horse is a maniac. You shouldn't be anywhere near him—not in the round pen, not in his stall, not ever!"

Her chest swelled, and her eyes narrowed rebelliously.

Her dark look only fueled his fury. "Don't you get it? Next time he'll kill you!"

"Not if you stay out of this barn and let me do my job!"

"Right! So, it's my fault? I have half a mind to report this to Mr. Collier."

"No! If I don't save him, Mr. Collier will kill him."

"Good."

"No! Please… He's better. I know he's still easy to startle, but he'll get even better. It's just going to take time and patience. He's been through a lot."

"He's a killer."

"Not many living creatures get the easy, pampered start in life you've had. That's why you can't possibly understand what it's like for the rest of us!"

Her lovely voice had softened with desperation and love for Wild Thing but it didn't hold a trace of self-pity. When her impassioned eyes misted, he noticed they were as beautiful as sparkling amethysts.

"I know you don't care what I think, but Lizzie loves him. Spare him for her sake!"

The girl was passionate, compassionate…and despite her ragged jeans and faded shirt, gorgeous, as well.

Damn those eyes of hers. Again they reminded him of jewels, with lavender facets of light and dark that made his blood run hot and cold. Those damn eyes, coupled with having held her too close for too long in a shadowy barn that afforded him the privacy to follow through on his desire, had him hard as granite. Aware of her soft, slim body pressed tightly into his, he didn't even try to defend himself from the heat that her sexy curves generated.

It would be so easy to take her right here.

Her mouth was full and luscious and suddenly he wanted to kiss her, to dip his tongue inside and taste her. Would she open her mouth and let him?

The heat in her gaze was generated from *some* emotion. Maybe she felt what he did.

"What?" She had gone still. Her eyes never left his face. "Let me go!" Her voice was shallow.

"You don't want me to do that, and you know it." In the grip of a need too fierce to deny, his voice was raspy.

His gaze moved hungrily lower. She had soft, lush breasts. Hell, he wanted way more than a kiss, and he wanted it very badly. She was Jesse Ray's daughter, so she probably wanted it, too.

Feeling justified in testing a girl of such easy virtue, he gripped her shoulders and pulled her closer. Before she could react, he lowered his mouth to hers so he could take his first taste of her. His lips were hard and demanding because he expected easy compliance. And for an instant she responded just as favorably as he'd imagined, by gasping and sighing and clutching him closer. Her lips did part, and he felt her tongue, if only for an instant. Then almost immediately she stiffened. Recoiling, she balled her hands and began to pound at his chest, thrashing wildly.

When he didn't immediately let her go, her face flushed with anger. "You wouldn't treat Lizzie like this! You wouldn't try to take her in a barn like she was something cheap and easy without ever even having a single conversation with her!"

"Well, you're not Lizzie Collier, are you? You're Jesse Ray's girl."

"And that makes me too low to have feelings like you and your kind? Well, I do have feelings! And I'm not like my mother, you hear! So, go find your precious, saintly Lizzie Collier, and leave me in peace! She's your girlfriend. Not me! And I wouldn't ever want to be!"

But the last was a lie. The quick tears of shame and desolation in her lovely eyes and the thick pain in her ravaged tone told him so. She wanted him, but on equal terms. She didn't want to be someone cheap in his eyes. Her pride, as well as her longing for him, tugged at his heart and made him feel ashamed even as it made his desire for her increase a thousandfold.

He hadn't misread her. She had wanted him, badly. But Jesse Ray's daughter had as much self-respect as Lizzie Collier did any day.

For a long moment, she gazed at him as if pleading for something he was at a loss to give even as her look tore his heart. Then, with a desperate cry, she pushed free of him and ran out of the barn. As he watched her retreating across the pasture, he was stunned by her grace and vital beauty and by how much more he wanted her than he'd ever wanted Lizzie. He was baffled by how low and ashamed he felt by that fact. She was just Jesse Ray's girl. Why the hell should he feel such an overpowering need for her, such a need to apologize to her?

For weeks afterward, he'd tried to put the scent and softness and taste of the spirited and unsuitable girl out of his mind, but she'd been too lovely, too passionate, too brave, too forthright—too sexy. He'd dreamed of her, dreamed of making love to her.

He tried to forget her, but then his friends began to tell him stories about Maddie—marvelous stories he'd hungered to hear. How Maddie raced with the other kids, mostly the boys, in the pastures outside town. How she always won on the back of that prancing demon, Wild Thing. They said that she'd tamed him, that she was fearless, that she would ride bareback, that the pair could jump anything.

Why, one day after school when Cole's friend Lyle had been smoking in his vintage Mustang with the top down, she and Wild Thing jumped over him and the car.

"Crazy horse came so close to my head I dropped my cigarette in my crotch. Burned a hole in my best pair of jeans," Lyle had complained.

Such stories had impressed Lizzie, but they'd merely proved to Cole that Maddie was a headstrong fool—and brave, stubborn and determined. Even if the older generation in Yella wouldn't change their minds about her because of her mother, some of the kids began to think she wasn't as bad as they'd been taught. Maddie was smart in school, too, and Miss Jennie, whose approval was hard to win, thought she was as good as anybody.

For all that, Cole knew his mother would never approve of Maddie as his girlfriend. After his mother had married into the legendary Coleman family, she felt her children had a position to uphold. Still, despite his better judgment, his fascination with Maddie began to consume him. Thus, it hadn't been long before Cole started coming home from the university every weekend to seek her out.

He'd go to the barn and watch her train Lizzie's horses, especially Wild Thing. Maddie worked hard, giving more than she should to that monstrous beast, who now behaved like a docile pet to please her. Not that she said "I told you so" when Cole admitted he'd been wrong about her horse-training abilities. She simply basked in his praise, and he'd realized how much she enjoyed being admired rather than scorned. She was sweet when he apologized for kissing her, too.

Cole broke up with Lizzie and, with immense determination, began to court Maddie—but secretly.

He decided the gossips were wrong. Although she resembled her mother physically, she had a different character. Yes, mother and daughter shared the same jet-black hair, the same smooth, pale skin and the same lavender eyes that could turn blue when impassioned. Yes, their curvy bodies and sensual natures had been designed by God to drive men wild. But unlike her mother, Maddie was sweet and true.

Then she'd jilted Cole for Vernon Turner and left town,

proving his assessment wrong. She was just as feckless and promiscuous as her mother.

If she was trash, why couldn't he forget her? Why did he care if she was back in Yella?

She doesn't matter anymore. Hell, she never should have mattered.

So why did every nerve in his body feel taut? Why was his heart racing at the possibility of seeing her again?

Women like Maddie Gray, women who roared into a man's life and then left him like so much roadkill when they'd finished with him, were a dangerous breed. A smart man learned his lesson the first go-round and steered the hell clear of them.

So why was he standing up and slinging his jacket over his shoulders?

Cole had about a million things to take care of on the rig, like dealing with that crooked driller. He didn't have time for an unscheduled trip to Yella. Nevertheless, he scooped his cell phone and the keys to his Ford Raptor off his littered desk. Then he grabbed his sweat-stained beaver Stetson and rushed out of his trailer. Scanning the well site, which reeked of acrid fumes, he hollered for Juan.

After the air-conditioned trailer, the thick summer heat felt suffocating. Briefly he informed Juan that there was a problem at Coleman's Landing, his family's legendary ranch on the southern tip of the Texas Hill Country. Cole said he had to get down there fast, but that he'd be back soon. He told Juan to get the water well drilled and to damn the expense.

Then Cole was in his truck. Tires spinning, gravel and dust clouds flying, he set off for Yella.

After three miles of graded dirt road, his tires hit the main highway. He drove down that straight stretch of asphalt through parched, open country of scrub oak, mesquite and huisache like a madman, hating himself for being so all fired up to see her. She'd ruined his life...or at least several years of it, and she'd hurt sweet Lizzie, too.

Lizzie had loved him with every bone in her body, but because of Maddie haunting him, hard as he'd tried, he hadn't ever been able to love Lizzie as he should have. Or at least he'd never craved her, if that sort of cravin' counted for love—not the way he'd craved Maddie, with every fiber of his being.

Even Lizzie's dying words had been about Maddie, and he'd hated Maddie for distracting him at a time when he should have been concentrating solely on Lizzie.

But he had to see Maddie again. Hopefully all he needed was closure to get her out of his system. Something about the way she'd left him six years ago—without even so much as a goodbye—bothered him.

He had to know how she could have been so unfailingly thoughtful and kind during their long-ago summer romance, how she could have loved him so sweetly that final afternoon in August—and then run off with trash the likes of Vernon Turner that same night.

Who was she: The bad girl her own mother and the town claimed she was? Or the sweet, pure girl he'd fallen in love with?

He hoped to hell he wasn't fool enough to chase after a dream again.

Two

If Maddie felt nervous and out of sorts just being back in Yella, she felt even worse to be chasing Miss Jennie's dog onto Cole's wooded land. What if Adam was wrong? What if Cole came back to town before he was supposed to?

She dreaded seeing him more than anyone else in Yella, which was ridiculous. How could his rejection and contempt still hurt so much after six years, when she'd told herself repeatedly that the past—that who she used to be—no longer mattered?

Maddie hadn't been back to Yella since the night she'd run away because there were too many memories here, both good and bad. For years, she'd made the future her focus and only rarely looked back. Besides, coming here meant she'd had to leave Noah, who was enrolled in a summer day camp on Town Lake, with a dear friend. She missed him, but she wouldn't have people here judging him because of her—or noticing how much he resembled Cole and putting two and two together.

She'd only come back now because she owed Miss Jennie for everything good in her life.

Maddie wiped her damp brow with the back of her hand. Had Yella always been this suffocatingly hot in the summer? Of course it had. She just hadn't noticed when she'd been a skinny, fearless kid wearing a thin T-shirt and shorts, running wild in the woods.

Today, with the sun beating down out of a bright sky, the heat felt thick and ferocious, and it wasn't even noon yet. Strands of her long black hair had come loose from her ponytail and stuck to her cheeks and neck. Her T-shirt and cutoff jeans felt as if they were glued to her perspiring body.

Still, despite the oppressive heat and humidity and a faint sense of uneasiness, she loved the scents and sounds of the woods. The smell of grass and dust, the chorus of insects that hummed along with the birds, made her remember some of the brighter moments of her youth. Long ago she'd ridden in these woods. Here, on horseback, a slim, despised girl had acquired the magical power that riding a powerful horse could bring. Riding had taught her to be brave and strong.

Most of all she remembered riding here with Cole.

Don't think about him.

Better to fret about her company's fundraiser than Cole. Even though she dreaded the annual event and the stress of dealing with wealthy donors, especially the women who knew how to dress and where to shop and where to lunch, she preferred worrying about all of that to thinking about Cole.

He'd rejected her, had made her feel more unworthy than anybody else here ever had. Why couldn't she simply forget him? Even after Greg had come into her life last spring—solid, reliable Greg, who didn't know her secrets, who approved of her and wanted to marry her because of who and what she was now—she remained confused about her obsession with Cole, who'd never seen her as his equal.

He'd rejected her soundly—so why couldn't she let him go? Why was she so afraid of seeing him?

When she'd fled Yella six years ago, she'd been too traumatized to ever imagine coming back. In Austin, she'd tried to better herself, tried to live down the mother who hadn't wanted her, the sorry trailer in Yella where she'd been raised, the terrible night that had driven her away. Most of all, she'd fought hard to be a better mother to Noah than her mother had been to her.

Not that juggling single motherhood while working full-time and going to college had been easy. Especially not when the nagging fear that she really was what everybody here had believed—no good—had remained.

Then, five days ago, just when she'd been on the verge of setting a date for her wedding to the man who valued her, Miss Jennie had called from the hospital and said she'd fallen. Miss Jennie was the one person in Yella who'd always believed in Maddie, the one person who'd been there when Maddie had been terrified and desperate. So, when Miss Jennie had mentioned she'd just love it if Maddie could come for a few days because her niece, Sassy, lived in Canada and needed some time to wrap up her affairs before she could fly to Texas, Maddie had agreed to come.

Not that Miss Jennie's neighbors hadn't all offered to fill in, but Miss Jennie had made it clear that she would prefer spending a little time with Maddie...if only that were possible. "Time seems more precious as you get older," she'd said, her voice sounding frail.

Still, since Miss Jennie had helped her relocate and had lent Maddie money to go to college, there was no way she could say no, even if it meant facing Cole and the prejudiced town.

Up ahead Maddie heard the jingle of dog tags. Just as she was about to call him, Cinnamon barked exuberantly from the sun-dappled brush. Her heart sank as she realized that he'd set off for the swimming hole on the Guadalupe River where she and Cole used to secretly meet. Where they'd made love countless times. Of all the places she would have preferred to avoid, the icy green pool beneath tall cypress trees on *his* land topped her list.

For here she could be too easily reminded of Cole, of their brief affair. Back then she'd been young and in love and filled with anticipation for their every meeting. She'd been so sure that he'd loved her and would love her forever, and that his love, once known publicly, would change other people's opinions and she'd gain the respectability she'd craved. Even when he'd insisted on keeping their relationship a secret from everyone important to him, especially his mother, she'd believed in him.

It had taken a crisis of the worst magnitude to make her see him for what he really was—a typical boy in lust out for a few cheap thrills with the town's bad girl, a boy who'd never respected her and couldn't be counted on to save her. No, she'd had to save herself.

Maddie had had six years to deal with the trauma of the past. She was all grown up now. She knew that life wasn't a fairy tale, that she needed to get over the hurt that Cole and his mother had inflicted on her.

The last thing she wanted or needed now was to see him again and reopen all those old wounds. If she were lucky, Cole would keep to his oil fields while she was here with Miss Jennie.

Maybe then she would escape Yella unscathed.

Three

Two hours after he'd left the drill site, Cole pulled up to Miss Jennie's white house on the edge of town where her property backed up to a corner of his own estate. Miss Jennie's house, with its sagging wraparound porch, was a sorry sight in the middle of an overgrown, brown lawn. Not that Cole's mind was on the lousy condition of her house and yard as he slammed the door of his big, white truck and strode up her walk.

He was a little surprised when Miss Jennie's fool of a dog didn't race up to him, yapping. Whenever Cole rode on this part of his ranch he usually ran into the mongrel. On hot summer evenings Cinnamon loved nothing better than lying on a shady rock along the bank where the river was spring-fed and icy cold.

That particular swimming hole had often been Cole and Maddie's secret meeting place.

All he could think of was Maddie.

He knocked impatiently, but when the screen door finally

opened, it wasn't a reluctant Maddie prettily greeting him, but sharp-eyed Bessie Mueller from next door.

Cold air gushed out of the house around her as she set fists on her solid hips. Her wrinkled face was brown from working outdoors. She had a way of standing that made her look bolted to the earth.

"Your mother told everybody you weren't coming home till tomorrow, so, what has got you planting your dusty boots on Miss Jennie's doorstep today?"

It went without sayin' that everybody in Yella knew everybody else's business.

"Ranch affairs," he drawled, hating the way the lie made heat crawl up his neck. "Is Miss Jennie doing okay?"

"She's just fine, but she's restin' for a spell. She's had so much company this mornin'—all male. She's plumb tuckered out."

"And Maddie Gray?"

Bessie grinned slyly. "Oh, so, it's *her* you've come to see... like every other man in town?" The knowing glint in her black eyes irritated the hell out of him. "Well, she's out looking for Cinnamon, if you have to know. That's why I'm here. I told Maddie it wasn't no use chasin' that mongrel. When that fool dog isn't barking loud enough to wake the dead, he's after my poor chickens or diggin' up my pansies. He always comes back—when he takes a mind to."

Like all mammals, human or otherwise, living in Yella, Cinnamon had acquired a reputation.

Cole tipped his hat. "You tell Miss Jennie I'll be back a little later, then."

If Maddie was chasing Cinnamon, he knew where to find her.

When Cole tugged lightly on the reins, Raider snorted and jerked his head, stopping just short of the small creek that fed the river where ancient trees grew in such dense profusion they were almost impenetrable.

"The brush is too thick from here on," Cole said, "so this is where I'll leave you."

On a hunch that Cinnamon would lure Maddie to the pool by the dam, he'd saddled his large, spirited bay gelding and set off.

Dismounting, Cole looped Raider's reins over a fallen log near the rushing water and left the horse grazing in the shade.

Pushing back a tumble of wild grapevines that cascaded from the highest branches of a live oak, Cole made a mental note to get his foreman to send a hand out to clip the vines before they smothered the tree. Then, as he stalked through the high brown grasses toward the emerald pool, memories of Maddie played in his mind.

He and Maddie had ridden these trails together. When they'd dismounted they'd often played hide-and-seek. How he'd loved catching her and pulling her slim body beneath his. She would smile up at him, her flushed face thrilled and trusting in the pink glow of a late-afternoon sun.

After she'd left, he'd posted signs that read No Trespassing and No Swimming.

At the sound of a dog barking, Cole's heart began to race. When he recognized Maddie's low, velvety voice, he went stone-still.

"We shouldn't be here. We're trespassing. But you don't care."

Stealthily he inched forward until he caught glimpses of dewy skin and ebony hair through the trees.

Sitting on the dam, dangling her long legs in the water, she wore nothing but a blade of wet grass on her left nipple and a pair of black thong panties. Her exotic face with those arched, slanting brows was lovelier than ever. Not that his gaze remained on her face. Her naked breasts and slender waist and her legs that went forever stole his breath.

He gulped in air while his heart thudded so violently he was sure she'd hear. He could turn and go, but why should he? He'd come here to find her, hadn't he?

Slowly she dipped a rag—no, it was her T-shirt—into the water and squeezed it so tightly that rivulets of sparkling liquid showered her throat and breasts.

"Ah, nothing like icy water on a hot day," she purred huskily as she put the T-shirt back into the pool and dripped more fluid diamonds over her body. "I was burning up."

The dog was panting hard. Cole was burning up, too, but his condition wasn't entirely due to the heat.

Erect, spellbound, he watched as the blade of grass got caught in the currents of water tracing down her smooth, gleaming belly before sliding down to her navel. When a slender fingertip plucked it off her skin, heat shot through Cole. His sex, hot and hard, swelled painfully against tight denim. When Cinnamon walked onto the dam and shook water all over Maddie, she screamed even as she giggled.

"You are all dog," she said huskily, but she laughed, teasing the mongrel rather than chastising him.

Damn her to hell and back for being so gorgeous and unnervingly sexy. She seemed sweet, too, just as she always had—the very essence of everything feminine.

But looks could deceive.

Even though he knew what she was, memories of the first time she'd lain with him struck him full force.

She'd been flushed and naked as she'd whispered she loved him and always would. She had begged him to take her.

He'd kissed her throat and stroked her hair. "Are you sure about this?"

"No matter what happens, I want it to be you…who's first, I mean."

For a long time, his hands had skimmed over her body, touching her, caressing her. She'd been so innocent and so infinitely precious to him.

Determined not to hurt her, he'd been gentle and patient even though his youthful hormones had been raging. Hell, he'd even told her he loved her, too. Worse—he'd meant it.

Don't think about it.

But how could he forget how tight she'd been, or how she'd held her breath so long after he'd entered her, she'd scared the hell out of him?

"Are you okay?" he'd whispered.

"Better than okay." When she'd pressed her soft mouth to his throat she'd sent him over the edge. He'd apologized, but she'd begun to kiss him again, and he'd hardened inside her almost instantly.

"I've had a crush on you for years," she said. "I just never thought you could care for someone like me."

"Well, I do."

"Sometimes I still have to pinch myself so I know I'm not dreaming."

Now, determined to push the bittersweet memories aside and regain control, he counted slowly...backward from one hundred to zero. Long before he reached zero, more memories bombarded him, each one sweeter than the last. Then he couldn't count, couldn't think, couldn't do anything but feel his testosterone-engorged body thicken.

More than anything, he wanted to touch her warm, velvet skin, to taste her sweet lips...just one more time. Maybe once he was sated, he would be rational enough to remember how shabbily she'd treated him.

As if she sensed him, she slid into the water, screaming because it was so cold, and then swam away from the dam, leaving a trail of graceful ripples flashing in her wake.

Instead of listening to the voice of reason that told him

not to play with fire, he strode down to the bank and stood above her in the long shadows of the cypress trees, watching her swim, willing her to turn and face him.

When she did, her face whitened with shock. "Cole! What are you doing here?"

The alarm in her slanting blue-violet eyes cut him to the quick. But still his tone was hard when he said, "I heard you were chasing Cinnamon on my land, so I came looking for you."

When her exotic face went even whiter, his own craven desire made his gut clench.

Without another word, she dived underneath the water and swam as far away from him as she could. When she finally came up, she crossed her hands over her breasts and scrambled behind the nearest rock. "I—I didn't mean to bother you!" she began, blushing furiously as she gasped for breath. "If I'd known you were in town—I would never have come here! Your brother, Adam… He told me you wouldn't be back anytime soon. I swear he did!"

"Didn't you see the No Swimming signs? A kid nearly drowned here a couple of years ago, after a flood. Cinnamon is not worth risking your pretty neck by swimming here alone."

"Okay. I won't do it again. If you'll just leave, I'll dress and go."

"The last thing I want is you dressed and gone."

The stark look of terror reappeared in her eyes. "Don't start!" she whispered. "Please—"

The shame and fear in her frantic gaze tore at his heart. He remembered how sensitive she'd been on the subject of her mother and how shy she'd always been about sexual matters, especially in the beginning. But she'd never been this skittish. Suddenly he wished he could take back the suggestive comment.

"Somebody told me a while back that you're a mother now...that you have a little boy..."

Her violet-blue eyes widened with even more fear. Why?

"I just meant that as a mother, you shouldn't take unnecessary risks—like swimming here alone."

"My son is no concern of yours!" Her voice was high and thin. "You made that very clear—"

"When did we ever discuss your son?"

"What?" She seemed to catch herself. "You're right. Of course you're right. I saw your signs. It's just that I'm upset because you startled me. I shouldn't have gotten in the water without a buddy. If you'll just leave, I'll get out, dress and go. Like I said." She had begun to shiver, and her lips were blue.

"You can swim as long as you like...now that I'm here to watch over you."

"I don't want you here watching over me." Her teeth were chattering.

"Right." He set his hot, insolent gaze on her.

"Cole, I'm...I'm freezing. If...you won't go, would you please turn your back so I...can get out and dress?"

"Okay, already." Halfheartedly, he turned his back.

Not trusting him, she hesitated. A moment or two later, he heard water splash on limestone, followed by the whisper of damp feet on grass and the breaking of twigs as she scampered across the rocks to retrieve her clothes.

When a low curse escaped her lips, he turned out of concern and was rewarded with another glimpse of her tantalizing breasts and thighs. His breath hitched as she struggled to push her slim arms through the knotted sleeves of her wet, tangled T-shirt. Absorbed in pulling on her jeans, she didn't look up and see that he couldn't take his tortured eyes off her.

When she'd fastened her cutoffs, she looked up. "You cheated," she said.

"Sorry."

"I guess I shouldn't wonder, since you'll always think I'm the kind of girl who doesn't deserve your respect." With an indignant frown she leaned down and secured the now-docile Cinnamon with a leash.

"Damn," he muttered, feeling guilty as well as angry.

That she could chastise *him,* for anything, when she'd jilted him for Turner, was gallingly unfair.

"Don't worry. I won't presume to trespass on your land again," she said almost haughtily.

"You can swim here anytime," he said coldly. "It's just that I'd prefer that you bring a friend with you the next time."

"Who? With the exception of Miss Jennie, people here don't really like my mother or me much. If you'll recall, I...I never had any real friends in this town."

"I hear eight men stopped by to check on Miss Jennie this mornin'."

"For your information, I wasn't ever who you thought I was or who they probably think I am. It's taken me a long time to believe in myself...after...after the way you and the town treated me."

"Oh, really? I find that surprising. For someone so sensitive and romantic, you sure as hell slept with me and then ran off with Turner without so much as a goodbye."

When her skin went as pale as the bleached limestone bank, he felt as if someone had kicked him in the gut. But even as she began to tremble, her eyes blazed.

"Believe what you want about me!" she whispered as she hugged her arms around herself. "I'm glad I don't have to care anymore." But her eyes belied her indifference.

When he'd left the rig today he'd sworn he wouldn't rehash the past, but now he had to ask. "Tell me why you ran off with him. You owe me an explanation."

"Once...I foolishly thought...maybe I did owe you. So, before I left, I called you to explain, remember?"

Fury that she would lie so carelessly swelled inside him. "The hell you did! You called me eighteen months later—when it was a little late, since I was already married to Lizzie!"

"No! I called you the night I left. But your mother answered the phone. She told me exactly what you told her to tell me, that she didn't want my kind in your life. So, excuse me if I didn't call you back. I had a lot on my plate. But my problems then are none of your business now."

"My mother? You talked to my mother that night?"

She nodded.

"I don't believe you! There's no way she could have resisted throwing such a call from you in my face!"

"I don't care what you believe. Do you deny that when I called you again, a year and a half later, you were even less receptive than she'd been that night? If you do, let me refresh your memory. You answered the phone and told me you never wanted to talk to me again! Then you slammed the phone down. At least your mother had the guts to talk to me!"

Her beautiful violet eyes shimmered with remembered pain, making a muscle in his gut pull. Her accusation about his mother didn't play. His mother, who had rigid views of social order, would have skinned him alive if she'd found out he had anything to do with Jesse Ray's daughter.

"The truth is—you waited a whole year and a half after you'd run off to call. Like I said, it was too late."

"Well, then let's leave it at that! You got married to a nice, respectable girl. Maybe I moved on, too. Okay?"

But it wasn't okay. Why were feelings that he'd suppressed for years suddenly so important to him?

"I told myself to leave it at that! And I did, as long as Lizzie was alive—for her sake. But now that she's gone and you're here, damn it, I want to know why you left me for Vernon without any explanation. All I knew was what your mother told everybody—that you'd flaunted yourself around Vernon to spite her and had run off with him for the same reason."

She whitened. Although she tried to hide her fear, he saw that her hands were shaking. What was she so scared of?

Then she drew herself up straighter, and her beautiful lips thinned with determination. It was as if she found some inner strength that enabled her to face him down.

"I—I wasn't myself when I left. After talking to your mother, I believed you were relieved to be rid of me."

Relieved? He'd been in so much agony he'd thought he was dying. When he couldn't get in touch with her, he'd been wild to find her, to talk to her. Wanting to hurt her now, as she'd hurt him then, he said, "I should have been relieved. Any sane guy would've been. You *were* your mother's daughter, in the end."

"Well, there you go," she whispered in a small voice. "Lucky you...to escape my clutches."

Her casually tossed comment pushed him over the edge. "Well, damn it, what if I wasn't smart enough to be relieved?" he growled, hating himself for not hiding that she'd held such power over him. Hell, she *still* held power over him as she stood there looking pretty and wounded and sexy as hell in the wet T-shirt that clung to her breasts. "When you ran off, I was worried sick about you."

"You were?" She bit her lip and looked away in confusion, as if what he'd said made no sense.

"I thought about you all the time. I didn't want to believe what your mother was saying without hearing your side," he said. "Every night I'd come out here and wonder how you could just disappear like that. I missed you, damn it! I wanted to know you were okay, at least, even if you were with Turner."

"Did you ever try to find me?"

"I wanted to. But, hell, my father got sick a week after you left. I was forced to take over the family businesses. On his deathbed he confessed to having another son...Adam. Mother couldn't accept him. I had a lot on my plate, too."

Something in his low tone got through to her because she whispered in a raspy, broken voice, "I'm sorry about your father. I didn't know. I was upset when I left...and too ashamed to call you again after your mother had so soundly rejected me."

"You sure as hell should have been ashamed."

"It took me a while to get over...what happened." Her eyes darkened with pain. "But when I finally called you again, you didn't want to talk to me. No—you were cold and arrogant."

Because he'd been afraid he'd break if he spoke to her, because he'd been trying to be faithful to Lizzie, damn it.

"I don't see why you're dredging all this up now, Cole."

Maybe because nearly a year had passed since Lizzie's death, and he finally felt free to pursue whatever the hell he wanted. Because Maddie was here, looking even lovelier and more vulnerable than before. His reaction wasn't logical. He knew that. But somehow his involvement with Maddie wasn't over. Seeing her again had thoroughly convinced him of that.

"So, what was in those letters you wrote me after I refused to talk to you?" he asked. He remembered too well signing for those two certified envelopes and then angrily tossing them in a drawer and telling himself he had to forget them.

Maddie gasped and lost even more color. "Didn't you read my letters?"

"No. I signed for them, but I couldn't read them, for the same reason I couldn't talk to you on the phone—because of Lizzie. Maybe someone like you can't understand this—but I would have felt like I was cheating on her if anything you said tempted me. Then she died, and I couldn't read them out of loyalty to her. She'd been my wife. What had you ever done—except jilt me for Turner?"

Maddie drew in a sharp, anguished breath. Licking her lips,

she swallowed hard. "Okay," she finally said. "You just signed for them…. Well, whatever I said in those letters can't matter now," she said. "You owe me nothing. And I owe you nothing."

"I'm beginning to see they're a piece in a puzzle I need to explore in more depth."

"No! The past, which includes you, doesn't matter now!" But her voice shook. "I—I was nothing to you."

"How can you say that and act like I mistreated you—when you ran off with Turner?"

"You should thank me. I set you free so you could marry your precious Lizzie and have everyone in Yella think the best of you. And that's exactly what happened."

He remembered resenting how anxious his mother had been to push Lizzie on him after Maddie ran off and his father died. Maybe marrying Lizzie because he'd been sad and lonely and overwhelmed, and because his mother and the whole town had thought they'd make a perfect couple, hadn't been the smartest thing he'd ever done. Not that he could tell Maddie that he'd made bigger mistakes than sleeping with her.

"What did you write in those damn letters?" he demanded, really curious.

"Nothing that could possibly matter now," she said, too casually. "I was young and foolish. Money was tight. My girlhood fantasy got the best of my better judgment. You know, poor girl wins rich boyfriend after all…lives happily ever after with him in his big, white, legendary ranch house… and then everybody in Yella looks up to her. Some foolishness like that."

"I think it's high time I finally read them. I'll be the judge of what's foolish."

Her brows flew together. "You still have them?"

"I threw them in a desk drawer, in my office, up at my big, white house, as you put it. They should be there…that is, if Lizzie put them back."

"Lizzie?"

"On her deathbed, Lizzie confessed she'd found them when she was tidying up in my office and had steamed them open and read them. She said she resealed them and put them back. She made me promise to read them after she was gone, said I owed you that. And then she said she was sorry, truly sorry, she hadn't told me about reading them before…but that she'd been too jealous to do so, too afraid of losing me. Imagine what a heel I felt like for having made her jealous over someone like you. Out of respect for her, I haven't looked for them since her death."

Maddie's gaze was fixed on Cinnamon. "Well, there's no need to read them now," she said softly. "I'll go…."

"I'm not finished," he said. "I told Lizzie those letters didn't matter, that they never had mattered, because I'd married her, and she'd been the most wonderful wife a man could wish for."

"You were lucky then," Maddie said wistfully. "I hope to be as lucky…someday soon."

He hadn't felt lucky. He'd felt guilt-stricken and low for never having loved Lizzie as she'd deserved because of Maddie.

"She always loved you. From the time she first saw you," Maddie said softly.

"Yes," he muttered, familiar guilt washing over him. He'd broken Lizzie's heart to pursue Maddie in secret. After that first kiss in the barn, he'd burned for the town's bad girl so fiercely, he hadn't been able to help himself.

And now Maddie was back, as beautiful as ever. He still wanted her.

"Maybe it's good we saw each other today, so we can face the fact that the past is over," she said. "I'm sorry I ran off without saying goodbye. I was young, immature…" Her voice was even and polite, the voice she would use to console or dismiss a stranger. "It's nice knowing you had a wonderful

marriage, and I'm truly sorry for your loss. It can't be easy…
even now. Cole, I wish you well. I truly want you to be happy."

"Thank you," he muttered ungraciously.

"Someday you'll find another woman. Maybe she'll remind
you of Lizzie. You'll have children, build a family together…."
Her voice grew choked and then trailed off awkwardly.

He didn't want to be reminded of Lizzie, who had been the
bride everyone else had believed would be perfect for him.
They'd made each other very unhappy. He'd remained lonely
even in marriage.

"Goodbye, Cole."

When Maddie turned to walk away, he watched her slim,
denim-clad hips swing and noted the way her damp T-shirt
clung to her back.

Just watching her move with liquid grace as she vanished
into the woods had his blood surging like fire in his veins.
His breathing felt shallow. He wanted to strip her, to hold her,
to kiss her. He wanted her naked and writhing with her legs
wrapped around his waist.

He wanted *her*—period. Longed for her.

He'd stay crazy if he let her walk out of his life a second
time. At the very least she still owed him some answers.

Four

The past, all her secrets, were supposed to be dead and buried. But Cole had her letters! And he'd never read them! He didn't know about Noah!

Cole hadn't rejected Noah as she'd believed. Instead, he hadn't read her letters because he'd wanted to stay true to his new bride.

All these years, everything Maddie had thought about him had been wrong.

She'd hurt him when she'd left him. Imagine that. As she fought her way through the woods, back to Miss Jennie's house, she wondered why it had never occurred to her that he might have felt that same shredding of the soul that leaving had caused her?

Because she'd had zero self-esteem. Because she'd been Jesse Ray's daughter and he'd been a Coleman, and she'd told herself he would believe the worst of her as her mother had.

Even so, she had tried to call him and explain before leaving Yella. She'd been so hysterical she had called his home, no longer concerned with revealing their relationship. His mother's cruel words would be forever branded into her heart and soul.

"You've got your nerve, Miss Gray. How do you know my son?"

"We dated. This summer. I need to talk to him."

"You dated?" Hester's voice had been shrill. "I don't believe you. Maybe…he felt some cheap sexual attraction, but if he'd had any respect for you, he would have brought you home to meet his family. My son loves Lizzie. And I thank God for that! John doesn't care about you any more than any of the men who've slept with your trashy mother have ever cared about her. You're so far beneath him, all you'd ever do is drag him down into the gutter where your kind lives. I warn you, if you don't let him go, my husband and I will do everything in our power to destroy you."

"That won't be necessary. Somebody else already did that," Maddie had whispered.

She blinked at the blinding white light sparkling through the trees and came back to the present. She didn't want to remember. It shouldn't matter that Cole hadn't known what Vernon had done to her or that he hadn't known about Noah. It was too late to include Cole in Noah's life because any contact with her son's father was too dangerous to her own well-being.

Still, as Maddie walked away from Cole, the pain in her heart was so great she barely felt Cinnamon twisting and tugging against the leash. Even though the woods were dappled with golden sunlight, she felt that she was stumbling through a dark void.

She couldn't afford to feel sympathy for Cole. No way could she let herself care about the young man she'd walked out on six years ago, or the wounded man he was now. Not when long-suppressed fears concerning her son gripped her.

Her work had taught her that lives were fragile, especially the lives of the ill, the elderly, the young, the learning disabled and the people like herself who'd experienced severe trauma and didn't have wealth or a supportive family. One false step, one stroke of bad luck, could lead to ruin. That was why she had to marry Greg, who had a good job and a stable, loving family. Together, if they worked hard, they would build a respectable life. The kind of life she'd always wanted.

The Colemans were rich and powerful. They could do a lot for Noah. But they considered her inferior. What if they decided to use their money and connections against her—to prove her unfit and take Noah away?

Maybe she didn't have their kind of money, but she had character and determination and a mother's fierce love. If she followed her plan, she could give Noah the wonderful childhood and bright future she'd never had. Then Noah wouldn't need the Colemans' money or their name.

But if Cole found out about Noah now, she might never be free of his family and the past. And she *had* to be free of him…because he too easily aroused all her foolish dreams of love and romance. It wasn't her fault he'd believed the worst of her and hadn't cared enough to read her letters. She'd made a life for her son without him, a life that would soon include Greg.

Even though she was more mature now, just seeing Cole today had her heart racing in a torment of confusion that included hurt, loss and hope, which was the most dangerous emotion of all. She couldn't let herself listen to his side and believe in those dreams again.

But what if he wasn't like his mother? What if he had loved her when they'd been together?

And she couldn't help feeling sympathy for Noah, who would never know his father, and for Cole, who wouldn't know his son.

Maddie's mind warred with her emotions.

She'd spent her whole life trying to prove she wasn't like her mother, but she couldn't deny the surge of excitement she'd felt in Cole's presence this afternoon. She still wanted him.

If he learned about Noah and became a part of their lives, would Cole tempt her to cheat on Greg, the very best of men, whose appeal paled in comparison to the virile and charismatic Cole?

Bottom line—for Noah's sake she needed to maintain a stable relationship with Greg. And that would be more easily achieved if she closed the door firmly on her past, and on Cole.

If only she could get her letters back before Cole read them. But how? She didn't dare mention them again because that would just intrigue him all the more.

Suddenly she heard his heavy boots crashing through the brush behind her.

"Maddie!" he yelled in that deep, possessive baritone that instantly made her blood buzz with a fierce, hot need that both thrilled and terrified her.

Stunned by the urgency in her own heart, she whirled, her gaze widening when his green eyes caught and held hers. She should keep walking, but somehow she couldn't when his desperately intent gaze refused to release her.

The past and its new truths couldn't matter.

But they did.

Stirred too deeply to deny her true feelings, she felt herself in a time warp. A warm breeze swirled the emerald trees around them, and she remembered all the times she'd seen him looking just like this before she'd run into his arms in these very woods as a girl. Back then she'd trusted him completely. Back then he'd been hers to hold and love, at least in secret.

Now, instead of the hurt and rejection she'd felt for so long, she was remembering brighter moments, remembering how he'd picked her up and spun her around, remembering how he'd spread a blanket across the lush grasses beside the river before drawing her down beside him, remembering how he'd stripped her slowly so he could make love to her. Always, always he'd been infinitely patient and tender. And so dear.

At the happy memories, blood pounded in her temples, bringing tumultuous excitement and the kind of wicked delight she'd never once felt for Greg, not even when he kissed her. Six years were washed away in bursting sensations of breathless joy and hot carnal needs that exploded in every one of her nerve endings.

She hadn't slept with anyone since she'd left Yella. It was as if she'd been frozen—until this afternoon...with Cole.

Why him? How could she still want him when he brought back the past and all the ugliness of her life here? Why couldn't it be Greg? She wanted to look forward, not back.

What was happening to her? How could she feel so powerless to fight her feelings for Cole when she knew she could never trust him with her heart or with her son?

"I'll always be Jesse Ray Gray's daughter."

"I don't care."

He looked as conflicted as she felt when he grabbed her by the wrists and spun her into his arms, hard against his body.

"I'll get you all wet," she cried.

"Feels good," he rasped. "What could be better than a wet woman on a hot day?"

She felt herself blushing. When she clumsily dropped Cinnamon's leash, the little dog yelped and dashed away. Not that she cared. How could she concentrate on the dog when Cole was holding her so close she was trembling? How could she resist the burning need in Cole's eyes, even though some tiny, sensible voice in her head pleaded with her to be more intelligent?

Greg. Marriage. Stability. Noah's future.

Greg will protect you.
Cole's mother promised to destroy you.

"Cole," Maddie begged as her breasts lodged snugly against his muscular chest. "Cinnamon… He'll get away."

Cole tugged her nearer so that her nipples peaked against the violent thudding of his heart in his warm chest. "He knows his way home."

For no special reason her gaze lingered on Cole's sculptured, sensual mouth.

Reluctantly, she laid her head on his shoulder and inhaled his dizzying, clean male scent and the lemony flavor of his aftershave. "Oh, Cole," she whispered on a rush of longing.

He needed no further invitation. Pressing his warm lips against her earlobe, he sighed. "Baby, you feel so good."

A delicious current raced in her blood. His mouth nibbling her flesh set off sparks even as the memory of his mother's words ate into her soul.

You're so far beneath him, all you'd ever do is drag him down into the gutter where your kind lives.

For a long moment, Cole simply held her tightly against his long, hard body. "You smell good, like the woods and the creek…like everything I love best."

Feeling cherished, she closed her eyes and fought to forget his mother's cruel assessment, fought to forget that he'd let her go when he'd promised to love her forever.

Stroking her fingers through his thick ebony hair, Maddie felt herself in a sensual dream. He was so tall and solid and hot. He felt so right. For the first time in years, everything seemed perfect. Had she been striving for all the wrong things, when all she'd ever wanted was Cole?

He's the enemy, the man who threw you and Noah away.
No. That wasn't how it was. His father died right after you left. You were gone. He was so sad and lost, he turned to

Lizzie. He'd wanted to be faithful to his wife. She could see that, understand it.

When Cole lightly brushed his mouth across hers, his sweet kiss scorched.

When she clung instead of resisting, his lips became hot and hard and punishing. Fire raced in her veins. Another girl, without her mother's genes, might have felt shame to part her lips and give herself so easily. But Maddie gloried in the wildness of his touch and the sweetness of his taste as he made a thorough exploration of her mouth.

When he held her and kissed her like this, she couldn't deny what she'd really wanted these past six years: him.

Grabbing her bottom, he thrust himself closer and rotated his hips against hers so that she could be in no doubt of his state of arousal.

"I want you," he whispered possessively. "You know that, don't you?" He sounded angry about it. "Damn it, I still want you! I couldn't stop, no matter how hard I tried! Not even when I was married!" he raged. "I wanted you even then."

She could empathize with his anger. Oh, boy, could she ever. Yet his anger hurt, too. He'd wanted to forget her, had married to forget her.

"I tried to forget you, too."

Her fingers twined around his warm neck and caressed his damp hair even as she pressed herself into him as wantonly as he was pushing against her. His body felt like strong, sun-blasted rock, and she was melting in his heat.

In an instant, the past merged with the present. She was no longer an inexperienced girl. This was now, and she wanted him as a mature woman craved her one true mate. She couldn't deny it any more than she could deny her next breath.

Six years and all the battles she'd fought to become a new, respectable, brave person, the kind of young woman who could be a proper wife to a professional man like Greg, were nothing compared to this primal need she felt for Cole.

But what did Cole truly think of her?

Would he always see her as the trampy daughter of Jesse Ray Gray? Did he merely lust for her in a raw, animalistic way? Wasn't that why he'd rejected her and married Lizzie?

Because of her doubts, she found the inner strength to spread her fingertips wide against his chest. Shoving lightly, she stumbled back a step. With a growl, he caught her and steadied her by slowly pushing her against the thick trunk of an oak tree. With the tree supporting their weight, he began to kiss her lips, her throat and her breasts, which were still slick and damp. Feelings of desire swamped her all over again.

When his greedy, exploring mouth followed a silky path from her breasts to her lips, he plunged his tongue inside. Once more everything was softening and melting inside her. All too soon, passion blurred her doubts, many though they were, and she was ablaze and needy for more of his loving, which felt true and right despite everything. Nobody but him had ever kissed her like this, made her feel like this. There was an honesty in such feelings, wasn't there?

Sensing her response and riding it, his kisses grew harder and longer and infinitely sweeter, and she drank deeply of him, stroking his tongue with hers, feeling as if she could never get enough. When he brushed his mouth over hers again, she kissed him back, and with every kiss her soul-devouring desire built.

He began to murmur to her in soft, mesmerizing tones, his love words both passionate and tender. She felt his erection jammed hard against her belly.

Oh, she wanted to tear off her clothes and his, too.

But when he pushed her wet T-shirt up and began to fumble with the fastenings of her bra, a rush of cool air against her naked belly and Cinnamon's wild barks made her shiver and push his hands away.

This is happening too fast. You're not good enough for him. His mother hates you. He married Lizzie. No matter what he says, he rejected you—and Noah, too. By not talking to you and by not reading your letters, he rejected you both.

His pointed red ears cocked, Cinnamon stood five feet away, quivering as he watched her intently. She fought to concentrate on the eager little dog instead of on Cole, because if she didn't quit thinking about all the things she wanted to do with Cole, she was going to be naked and lying flat on her back underneath him, her legs spread wide, writhing like a wanton. No doubt, when he finished his business he would blame her and think her as cheap as her mother.

"We have to stop," she whispered, feeling miserable because she ached from wanting him. "Or we'll go too far... and regret it."

"I won't regret it."

He popped her bra loose with a snap. Lifting her breasts to his lips, his warm mouth licked each of her nipples until they beaded like a pair of ripe berries, causing tremors to race down her spine. Had she ever felt so weak and feverish and needy?

She pushed at him in earnest. "We have to stop this—now."

"What?" he muttered. "You can't be serious."

"I am!"

She felt desperately close to the edge. She shook her head even as her arms clung to him fiercely. "We have to stop," she whispered brokenly. "I'm begging you."

His eyes closed for a long moment as if he were trying to shut out her demand.

"Cole!"

"All right, then," he said at last. Giving her a dark, tortured look, he yanked his large, tanned hands from her body as well as his gorgeous lips from her breast. "You win."

Never in her whole life had she wanted anything more than she wanted him. She ached everywhere and all her nerves felt raw. Because her limp knees would not have supported her otherwise, she sighed heavily and leaned back against the tree. He looked so dark and bereft and handsome as he finger-combed his black hair, she had to sag against the tree for fear she would hurl herself back into his arms and beg him to take her.

Breathing hard, he turned his broad back on her and stared with weary frustration at Cinnamon and then at the sparkling river. For her part, she continued to lean against the tree trunk while she fought a losing battle to steady her breathing. After a long time, she pushed away from the tree and refastened her bra.

When she'd rearranged her clothes and smoothed her wet hair and was almost able to speak in a normal tone, she said, "I'm sorry about what nearly happened. I shouldn't have let things get so out of hand."

"It was my fault as much as yours," he growled moodily. "So, how long do you figure on being in town?"

"Why should that matter? This proves we need to steer clear of each other."

"I don't see it that way. I'd like to see you again. The sooner, the better."

"Not a good idea."

"Why?"

She just shook her head. "That's pretty obvious."

"What if I give you my word that I won't touch you? At least, not unless you ask me to."

Too aware of her own burning hunger, she stared at him.

"Look, there are things about our past I'd like to resolve," he said. "Maybe then we could both forget about each other. That's what we both want—right?"

She was so out of control, she didn't know what she wanted anymore. No. That wasn't correct. She wanted the life she'd planned, didn't she? So, why did denying him hurt so much she ached?

It was dangerous sport looking at man like Cole, a man who was still as wrong for her as he'd been in the past, especially when she was wet and trembling from his kisses. His stormy green eyes and tousled black hair made him look hot and turned on even while his uncanny resemblance to their precious son tugged at her heart...and her conscience.

At the thought of Noah, she flushed guiltily and shook her head. "We need to avoid each other."

"I swear I won't touch you." Cole's angular face was set, his low tone sincere. "Please—I really think we should see each other again. Do you think it's going to be easy for us to forget, if we walk away—after that kiss—when what we need is closure? We need to talk."

Even though she didn't feel at all sure of herself, she agreed with him. "Maybe you have a point."

"So let's ride and then have dinner at my house or have a picnic somewhere later this afternoon. You still like to ride, right?"

She'd always *loved* to ride. "You mean horses?"

"What else?"

In spite of herself, she brightened. "I'm afraid I haven't ridden much since I left Yella."

"Some things you don't forget." His eyes were on her lips as his words lingered in the charged air that separated them. "You always said you wanted to see my house and horse barn, but that wasn't possible...when my mother lived there."

"She's moved?"

"Yes. When my dad was dying, he told me about my

brother, Adam. I felt betrayed at first, of less importance to my father somehow. But I hid my feelings and drove to where he lived and met him. I asked him to come to Yella to help me manage the ranch so I could devote more time to the oil business. Mother didn't want me to have anything to do with Adam. She felt betrayed even though Adam had been conceived before she met Dad and without Dad's knowledge. She blamed Adam for the whole mess, and then me for accepting him. That's when she moved out of the house."

Maddie could understand Hester's feelings, but the mention of Cole's mother's intolerance dampened her spirits—and reminded her of what was at stake. If she went to his house, maybe she'd find a way to get back her letters, which he'd said were in his desk in his home office, without him ever having read them. Maybe she could secure her future.

Be honest. Really, you just want to see his house and spend a little more time with him. "Okay," she whispered faintly. "You win."

"How early can you get away?" he asked.

"I'll have to check with Miss Jennie."

"Good. Mind if I tag along?"

"If you do, Bessie will tell everybody. Your mother will probably know in five minutes flat that we were in the woods together."

"So what?" Smiling, he called to Cinnamon, and the maddening dog ran right up to him.

"He never does that when I call him!"

Casually Cole grabbed the leash and then laid the leather strap in her outstretched hand. His fingers brushed hers, causing a familiar jolt of heat that had her jumping back.

When he laughed, she scowled and kept a wary distance from him the whole way to Miss Jennie's. Even so, his striding grandly beside her in his boots and Stetson made her tension build.

Inside the house with him, it was even worse. Just knowing that he was lounging indolently in the parlor waiting for her to figure out a schedule had Maddie unable to settle, much less focus on her routine chores. She dropped things, and forgot what she was doing in the middle of a task.

The lean male figure sprawled on Miss Jennie's spindly ottoman was turning her life upside down, and she was powerless to stop him.

When her cell rang and she saw it was Greg, she declined his call.

"Who was that?" Cole demanded in a steely tone.

"Nobody important," she said, blushing.

"You're dating someone?"

"I don't want to talk about him."

He frowned as if the mere thought of another man in her life made him feel possessive, which, of course, he had no right to be.

"What about you? Are you dating?" she asked.

"No. When Lizzie died I told myself I wouldn't date for a year…which is nearly up, by the way."

"Oh…."

She was so mixed up. Usually she looked forward to Greg's calls. Usually she loved having him tell her about his morning and sharing her own with him.

Guiltily she remembered Cole's kisses on her mouth and breasts. Just thinking about them brought the butterflies back to her tummy and made her feel as wildly alive as an infatuated teenager.

Her pleasure in Cole's possessiveness and her disloyalty to Greg only increased the confusion she'd been feeling earlier.

What was happening to her?

Five

There was no telling what the neighbors had made of her wet hair and wet T-shirt when she'd returned to Miss Jennie's with Cole. So Maddie felt both light-headed and mortified when she left Miss Jennie's on Cole's arm later that afternoon. Not that he seemed to care what Bessie and her ilk thought about them being seen together.

He'd insisted on returning to Miss Jennie's in his truck to pick her up, after he'd taken his horse back to his house. And now, while he strode confidently to his truck, she kept her eyes glued to the sidewalk. They were almost to his big, white pickup when she saw Bessie's window shade move.

In a deliberate attempt to downplay her looks, Maddie had coiled her glossy black hair into a severe knot at her nape. She'd buttoned her white blouse to her neck and had secured its cuffs at her wrists. Her lips were pale because she hadn't bothered to freshen her lipstick. Her jeans were tight, but she'd brought only one pair.

"Bessie's watching us," she murmured.

Without bothering to so much as glance in Bessie's direction, he opened Maddie's door.

"She's probably already told everybody we went skinny-dipping," Maddie said.

His dark eyes traced her curves. "I wish you'd suggested that when we had the chance."

"No sexual innuendo. You promised!"

"No, I promised not to touch you."

"Innuendo leads to touching...."

He smiled. "You're saying there's hope."

"I'm saying don't!"

"Then stop tempting me by blushing so charmingly."

"There you go again!"

"Look, you're not committing a crime...just because you're beautiful. You could dress sexier. That wouldn't be a crime either. Hell, it's a bigger crime that you don't."

Her breath caught. Did he want to kiss her again as much as she wanted his mouth on hers?

Don't even think about it, or look at his lips, because he'll see how much you want him.

When he climbed inside and started the truck, she snapped on her seat belt. The nearness of him and the faint scent of his lemony aftershave made her blood quicken and her hands tremble. As they sped toward his ranch, her pulse beat unsteadily just because he was beside her.

When he sucked in a long breath, she realized he was on edge, too.

"It's really hot," she said.

"It's July."

They made a few more inane remarks about the weather and climate change before lapsing into a silence that lasted until they reached his house.

The Colemans had long been a respected family in Texas,

so naturally, like everybody else in town, she'd always wanted to see his grand yet informal house up close. But since he'd never considered her part of his world, he'd never issued an invitation.

As a girl, all she'd managed to catch were glimpses of his big, white house with its columns and wide verandas from her secret hiding place in the brush. How she'd admired the house and the barn and the swimming pool and tennis courts where she'd watched him play tennis with Lizzie. A paved road wound past grassy paddocks where horses sometimes grazed.

How different today was now that she was formally invited. How excited she felt when he parked at his front door and let her out in full view of his wiry foreman, Joe Pena. Not that some of her high spirits weren't dashed when the older man's weathered face blanched after Cole asked him to saddle Raider and a suitable mare for them to ride later.

"Miss Gray hasn't ridden in six years, so maybe Lily would be perfect," Cole said.

Joe smiled affably enough at Cole, but his jaw hardened whenever he looked at her. "Thank you," she said to Joe.

Without a word to her or a glance in her direction, the man turned his back on her and marched stiffly toward the barn.

Her mother had slept with Joe once or twice, and that had caused a rift in his marriage.

Cole took Maddie's arm gently. "Don't mind Joe," he murmured as he swept her up the stairs and inside his house.

"It's hard to forget that here I'll always be Jesse Ray Gray's daughter."

"It's way past time you grew a thicker hide."

"How—when all it takes is a dark look or a remark to bring it all back?"

"If you want me to follow him to the barn and invite him to a boxing match, I will."

"No."

"Good, because it's too hot for a boxing match. So forget about Joe and his stupid prejudices."

It was difficult when she knew his prejudices were well-founded.

The minute Cole shut the front door behind them, she felt as if she were in another, more privileged world. He pointed to a low table near a window and said she could set her purse down.

After doing so, she smiled in appreciation as he led her through a series of pleasant, oak-paneled rooms with tall ceilings, rooms that generations of women in his family had filled with antiques, Texas memorabilia and family history that included many pictures of the Colemans socializing with famous Texans and various presidents.

How did it feel to have a family you could be proud of?

She felt nothing but shame as she remembered the stench of her mother's trailer and the garbage-strewn lot it had shared with another even sorrier trailer on the edge of town. Had her mother ever taken a single photograph of her? The only pictures she had of herself were tattered school pictures that Miss Jennie had given her.

Here photographs of friends and family were abundantly displayed on walls and shelves. When his mother's likeness glowered at her from a beige wall, Maddie flushed with guilt. Did his mother already know he'd stopped by Miss Jennie's to see her?

"As you can see, Colemans aren't good at throwing stuff away," he said.

"Because you have a history to be proud of."

When his cell phone rang, he pulled it out and frowned. Instead of answering it, he said, "I'm turning this off. Damn thing rings all the time."

"Who was it?"

"My mother."

"Go ahead. Talk to her. I don't care," she lied.

"Later." He punched a button or two and slid it back into his pocket. "There—for now it's off."

Maddie couldn't help grinning a little triumphantly at his mother's stern picture before she began a study of the formal photographs and the painted portraits of his ancestors that filled his den. These were Noah's ancestors, too. She felt a pang of guilt that her son would never know about them.

Pushing Noah to the back of her mind, she imagined Cole spending his free time in this masculine room with its dark carpets and huge reddish-brown leather sofas and matching armchairs. How often had he brought other women here? Women he'd respected? Women he'd introduced to his mother?

He joined her, telling her again what she already knew, that the ranch had been put together shortly after Texas had won its independence from Mexico, and that during the Civil War, Yankees had burned the first house.

"This second, much grander structure was built after the family recovered. It faces due south just like our state capitol in Austin—for the same reason, to spurn the north and the 'damn' Yankees."

She managed to laugh lightly. "I hadn't heard that before."

"Like most Texans, we're a stubborn, proud bunch," Cole said, not bothering to hide his pride in his family and his state.

Cole's ranch house was lovely, classy. Once when she'd lain in his arms she'd foolishly dreamed of living here, of being accepted because she was his wife.

But the town and his mother would never have approved, so he'd turned his back on Maddie and had married Lizzie. As proof of his brief, joyous union with his wife, he kept several informal photographs of her on the tables and shelves. And in every one of them, sweet, blonde Lizzie was looking up at Cole's rugged, tanned face with adoring blue eyes.

Maddie lifted one of the photographs. "She looks so happy and in love."

Without a word, he took the picture from her and placed it facedown.

"She's gone now."

Maddie winced at the rejection she felt in his icy tone. She couldn't help remembering Miss Jennie telling her how worried the whole town had been because Cole had stayed drunk for six months straight after Lizzie's death.

"His mother says he'll never get over her," Miss Jennie had said. "They were high school sweethearts, you know."

Until a stolen kiss in a barn had temporarily awakened his lust for the town's bad girl.

In spite of everything, Maddie had felt genuine sympathy for him in his time of loss.

"She always loved you so much," Maddie said gently, knowing now that all he'd ever felt for her was lust. "Since she was a little girl."

"Yes," he muttered coldly.

"The whole town wanted you to marry her and give them their happy ending. And you did."

"Can we talk about something else?" Again his expression was grimly forbidding. "Look, I didn't bring you here to talk about Lizzie." A nerve jerked in his cheek. "All that's over now." He took her arm and led her toward the open door of what was obviously his office. "You haven't seen the rest of the house yet."

Forgetting his promise not to touch her, he took her hand and led her inside the room. Her quick shiver brought a wicked glint to his eyes, but he let her go without teasing her.

"This is where I work. Sloppily, as you can see."

Stacks of papers littered the top of his massive mahogany desk and spilled out of its drawers.

Her mind on the letters now, she gazed at the drawers, barely listening as he explained his various businesses to her.

There was the ranching operation to run, he told her, the other heirs who didn't live on the ranch to satisfy, several farms to deal with, his mother to cater to, his ongoing oil and gas business, which was booming and kept him away from the ranch, his beloved horses, and several other income streams to keep track of. Ranching, he said, was a difficult business due to the unpredictable nature of so many important variables such as the weather and the price of feed and cattle. His father had been on the brink of bankruptcy when Cole had taken over. He was still in the process of streamlining the cattle operation and diversifying into other, more lucrative businesses.

"We got lucky with this new oil and gas play," he said. "I've hired geologists and drillers, and am constantly expanding. There's so much exploration going on in Texas, I can't get the men or the parts I need. Or even the frac water to drill..."

Her gaze skimming the drawers, she listened absently while he told her about a greedy water-well driller. All but the bottom one were open.

"But I've been rambling, and you're studying my messiness instead of listening," he said, reaching for her and then dropping her hand when she jumped, startled at his touch.

"Sorry—I keep forgetting about the no-touching rule!"

Caught off guard and feeling slightly ashamed because she imagined he still saw her as an easy woman, Maddie jammed her hands into her pockets. "It's all very interesting," she murmured.

That was when she saw his arrowheads, which were framed and mounted above his desk. Much to her surprise, the ones she'd found near their secret pool and had given him were in the center of a collection he'd arranged in the shape of the state of Texas.

"Your arrowheads. You even framed the ones I gave you."

"Yes. You were always so patient and observant when we searched those old Indian mounds. I was too easily distracted."

He was staring so intently at her lips that she blushed.

"So, what do you feel like doing?" he said too abruptly, glancing outside. "Are you hungry?"

"Not yet," she whispered, suddenly feeling ill at ease and shy around him.

"Do you want to ride now? Take a picnic along for later?"

Riding was a rare treat since she couldn't afford her own horse. Thrilled at the thought of riding anywhere again, much less with him, she nodded. She'd worry about the future and what was best later. Later she'd find an opportunity to search for her letters.

She helped Cole pack ham sandwiches, chips, fruit, cookies and canned drinks before they headed out to his barn. As they approached the tall, red building, an Australian shepherd bounded out of it, wheeling between them, greeting them with exuberant barks. The dog jumped, licking her hands, sniffing her jeans. Laughing, Maddie knelt and let it lick her cheek, too.

"Why does Bendi get all the kisses?" Cole asked when she remained at the dog's level.

"Bendi, is that your name, fella? Bendi may be my only friend in Yella...besides Miss Jennie," she said, stroking the dog.

"What about me?"

"We weren't really friends, now were we?"

"I always liked you," he whispered.

"You never brought me here...the way you brought all the rest of your real friends."

"My mother and dad lived here then."

"See what I mean. I was always Jesse Ray Gray's daughter, so you were ashamed of me."

His face darkened. "With my mother, it was difficult. She was always so critical, and she had about a hundred rules she lived by. Maybe I wasn't ready to tell her about you. About us. Maybe I was too afraid she'd spoil it, or drive you away. Maybe I didn't realize how you'd see it and feel about it." He paused. "I never meant to hurt you."

"Look, I don't want to quarrel about the past. We have our own lives now, don't we? Let's just ride and enjoy what's left of the afternoon."

She rose from the ground and headed toward the barn in silence with the dog racing circles around her.

"If coming here was so important to you, you could have asked me to show you the house," he said defensively behind her.

Since she didn't want to argue, she just kept silent.

Except for Bendi's toenails scraping the concrete inside the barn as he trotted happily beside her and the sounds of horses munching grain and corn in their stalls, the shadowy barn was silent. In the tack room, saddles, bridles and halters hung from whitewashed walls. Everything—the sink, the desk that held a telephone, the floor—was immaculate.

The two horses that Cole had ordered to be saddled nickered as he opened the first stall door. Horseshoes rang on the concrete as he took the reins of a lovely palomino mare with brown eyes and led her out.

"Meet Lily. She's gentle and likes everybody."

"She's lovely."

At the compliments, Lily lowered her golden head and let Maddie stroke her.

"Good girl." Maddie held out the apple she'd brought and enjoyed the feel of the mare's lips and nose as she eagerly took a bite.

Horses—they'd been her salvation as a girl. If it hadn't been for horses and Miss Jennie, where would she be now?

Maybe in some shabby trailer enduring some awful man's abuse. Or worse, abusing her own child.

Cole opened another stall and led out a tall bay gelding. "And this is Raider. He and I go way back. He's half Arab and half quarter horse and pretty challenging to ride."

"In what way?"

"He doesn't like white rocks. And he insists on bossing all the other horses. He thinks he should decide which hay pile the horses can eat, and if they don't agree, he lays his ears back and charges them."

"Oh, dear." She began to stroke him. "A big boy who doesn't play well with others. In my line of work I meet a lot of people with your problem."

"Lily is so agreeable that he isn't threatened, so he doesn't get up to many of his bad tricks when he's around her."

Outside, the wind rustled in the trees. Raider stomped, snorted and tossed his head, eagerly anticipating their ride.

Cole gave Maddie another moment to stroke and talk to Lily. Then they mounted and headed for the narrow, shady trail that wound through the brush. "I keep the trail groomed in the summers, just for riding," Cole said.

"Do you ride often?" she asked wistfully, unable to imagine such a luxury.

"I've been away a lot overseeing my rigs and haven't had time when I'm here, so getting out today will be fun, especially since you'll be with me." His words, warm and seductive, sang along her nerve edges.

Don't say things like that. Don't make me long for what I can never have.

"Riding will be a special treat for me, too. As a single mom, I don't take off much time for myself."

The sky was a deep blue, and the clouds against the horizon looked as soft as huge tufts of cotton. The light breeze curling the grasses made the late afternoon cooler than expected.

Maddie, who rode behind Cole, found herself enjoying the ride more than she'd enjoyed anything besides Noah in years.

He set off on a gallop. Laughing aloud, she raced after him across one of his endless pastures with her hair streaming behind her. Her blood tingling from the thrill of it, she felt like a girl again with the big animal beneath her. When Cole turned and their eyes met, excitement charged through her in a white-hot jolt. Later, when he pulled up on his reins and headed in the direction of the river, she followed.

"The ground is not firm enough here to gallop," he said as he waited for her to come alongside him.

She wasn't surprised when Cole chose the pool where he'd discovered her earlier that day as their destination to water their horses and picnic.

When Cole helped her dismount, she stood beside Lily, stroking the horse, pretending she felt as calm as the mare, who dipped her mouth into the pool and drank through golden lips.

Cole opened a cold beer can and offered it to Maddie. When she accepted it, he popped the top off a tonic water and lifted it to his sculpted mouth. Studying his dark, angular face, especially his mouth, and the reflections of the trees and sky in the green water, she fought to pretend she felt nothing for him. But her blood was buzzing even before she drank deeply.

"So, who are you now, Maddie Gray?" he whispered as he led her to a limestone rock that served as a bench. "Now that you're all grown up and educated? What have you made of yourself?"

"My story is probably pretty ordinary."

"Not to me."

"I don't have your lineage of famous pioneer Texans. I was just a child here, going hungry on occasion and feeling trapped in that awful trailer with Mother when she was there.

And when she wasn't, I was always too scared of the neighbors in the next trailer to play outside."

He frowned as if he genuinely empathized with the child she'd been. "You don't have to talk about it."

"You asked," she said, touched by his response. She'd never talked about these things with him before. Or with Greg, she thought. Greg knew next to nothing about her past, and she didn't want him to. For some reason that she didn't understand, she felt like talking to Cole this afternoon. Since they both needed closure, maybe telling him as much of the truth as she dared would help.

"Yes. Maybe it's time I did talk about it. Mother didn't come home lots of nights—sometimes she'd be gone several nights in a row. Out on dates, I suppose. Dates that lasted all night…and sometimes several days. I would hide in the closet even though I was scared of the dark."

"Did you ever tell a teacher that you were so scared you locked yourself in a dark closet?"

"Only Miss Jennie, when I was in high school. She took me home with her one afternoon. Everything was so clean and bright and nice in her house, and she was so gentle and kind that I started to cry because I wanted to live in a place like hers, with no smudges on the walls, a place with tablecloths and clean sheets on the beds, a place where I felt safe and where people were kind. Mother, you see, always screamed and cursed at me. Most people in Yella treated me like they hated me, too, though not Liam or Lizzie, who were always nice to me. So, I never imagined that I might achieve a decent kind of life.

"But Miss Jennie gave me hope. Until I started spending afternoons at her house in high school, my only friends had been horses."

"What was the name of your first horse pal?"

"Remember how our trailer was next to Jasper Bower's

property? Well, Mr. Bower noticed that I used to bring his two horses apples after school. He was the one who gave me my first job mucking stalls in exchange for riding lessons. He let me take care of Pico and his other horses and gave me a good reference and that led to other jobs. I loved being in barns and working with horses, but until Miss Jennie saw how lost I was and befriended me, the human world mostly seemed big and unfriendly. And I felt helpless to ever change anything. She made me realize that if I didn't want to be despised my whole life, I couldn't hide out in barns. It was up to me to make something of myself. She'd been poor, too, you see, and she told me how she'd changed her life. She set out a very specific path to follow, with steps and options. We made a plan for what I'd do after graduation. I swore that if I ever succeeded, I wouldn't forget that there were other little girls like me who didn't have anyone to turn to, and that I'd help them...just like she helped me."

"And? Have you?"

"I try so hard. I try every day. I got my bachelor's degree in sociology and psychology so I could work at the same homeless shelter that took me in when I left Yella. Now, on cold days, I have coats to give shivering children and diapers for wet, dirty babies and bus tokens for poor mothers who need transportation to get to work. I run a day care for children and a shelter for women and children. And one for disabled men, as well. We feed lunch to three hundred people a day. I feel like the shelter I work for makes a difference."

"You make the difference." His gaze was so intense with interest and admiration, it caused a warm rush of pleasure and pride to swamp her.

"Working with these people requires many of the same skill sets I acquired training horses. Only you're dealing with people. With rules, patience, determination, compassion and a plan, you can sometimes work miracles." She paused. "When

Noah's older, I need to go back to school for my master's so I can do more. But right now I need to be with him as much as I can. Children grow up fast. You don't want to waste a moment."

"If I had a son I'd feel the same way."

Her head jerked. When her eyes met his, his warm, thoughtful gaze unnerved her.

"I'm sure you would," she whispered haltingly.

For a second or two she was so connected to him she felt she had to tell him about Noah—because it was the right thing to do. She caught a panicky breath. Thankfully, he looked away, and in doing so, broke the spell. Squeezing herself, she let out a sigh. She had to be careful. Confiding in him had made her feel closer to him, and that closeness was dangerous.

As the sun turned golden-red and the sky blazed, he continued asking her questions. So eager was she to answer them she barely noticed the lengthening shadows as the sun sank lower.

After she finished her second beer, he unpacked their sandwiches and chips, which were delicious. Since they were there, she ate too many cookies, which he teased her about after she lamented having done so.

"Lighten up on yourself," he said. "It's easy to know what you should eat, but not always so easy to eat what you should. Besides, what would the world be coming to if Yella's number one bad girl lived up to her virtuous ideals one hundred percent of the time?"

As she laughed, she found it amazing and scary that she could feel so easy opening up to him. It was as if he were a true friend of the heart, instead of what he really was to her— the rich college boy who'd once lusted for her body and the powerful man who could threaten her future if he discovered her secret.

"Do you ever save any adults?"

"A few. We are connected to all the agencies in town that

can help them with their special problems. If you're a person who's down and out, and you want to change, we can teach you how to get your medications, how to fill out a job application or an application for an apartment. But a person has to be fiercely determined to succeed. There are so many basic skills functioning adults require…like money management and taking care of health issues."

In his turn, Cole talked about his oil and gas company and his ranch. She got a little lost when he tried to explain a modern drilling technique called hydraulic fracturing. Fracking, he explained, involved using pressurized water, sand and chemicals to extract more gas and oil from rock formations than had previously been possible. "But I'm not saving lives," he said. "I'm just making money."

"The modern world can't survive without energy. You saved the ranch, your family's heritage."

"There's that." He smiled. "Hey, the sun's going down fast. We better ride back to the house before it gets totally dark."

When he helped her remount Lily, her spirits rocketed at his nearness and his casual touch. As she stared down at his handsome face, which was half in shadow, she felt her stomach flutter. His intent gaze lingered on her, as well, increasing her nervousness. He didn't have to touch her to be dangerous.

For years, she'd been crushed by loneliness and the hard work required to pull herself up from nothing. Even now that she'd found Greg, she often felt lonely. Why did she never feel as connected to Greg as she felt right now to Cole?

How can you think that when you know Greg wants you as a person and Cole wants you for only one thing?

Instead of feeling outrage over Cole's lust for her, a delicious shiver of excitement coursed through her. Was she as shameless as her mother?

She had to stop this. She had to get back to his house and find her letters and go.

Not long after they remounted and headed back to his home, a full moon rose, painting the landscape with shimmering silver. Beside Cole, her blood began to pulse in ever-deepening awareness of him. When they reached the barn, which loomed in the dark, and he lifted her down, she was already so hot for him that she couldn't prevent herself from trembling when her body slid briefly against his.

No sooner were her feet on the ground than she sprang free of him.

Not that she felt much safer standing several feet away. How could she when all she wanted was for him to wrap her in his arms again and kiss her?

Breathing hard, he stared down at her so hungrily her own mouth watered. "You said not to touch you."

"Yes…."

"Then don't look at me like that."

When she didn't stop, he closed his eyes on a groan. His massive chest swelled, and he rasped in a harsh breath. "We'd better put the horses up," he said, his voice biting as he heaved out another violent breath.

For no reason at all she was too shy and tongue-tied to utter a coherent thought.

She should never have come out with him today or talked to him so openly, baring her soul, so to speak. Maybe then she wouldn't have reawakened all those dangerous yearnings and unrealistic hopes that had haunted her for years. She'd always wanted more from him—so much more than he'd ever been able to give to a girl he'd considered beneath him.

She knew too well that theirs was an impossible relationship.

But tonight he'd brought her to his house, talked to her about his family and work, listened to her with respect.

None of that should matter. She should stick to her decision and marry Greg and have nothing more to do with Cole.

But that was a difficult plan when Cole made her feel so alive.

Six

Since her heart was in shreds just from spending a pleasant evening with Cole, she wished she could forget her letters and demand that he drive her home. But when Cole turned on the lights in the barn and neither Joe nor a groom appeared, the smell of hay and the soft nickering of the horses seduced her into offering to help him put both horses to bed.

Together they removed the saddles and bridles and carried them to the tack room. Together they hosed down the horses, rubbing their long, narrow faces with big puffy sponges, squeezing the sponges repeatedly so that the water ran down their great bodies and legs and gurgled in the drain.

"I've missed working with horses," she said. "Horses don't lie to you, so they don't break your heart as often as people do."

His eyes studied her face for a long moment. He'd hurt her, made her feel cheap and unimportant to him. Maybe he

hadn't done it deliberately, but he'd hurt her just the same.
For six long years she'd carried those scars.

"I'm sorry you had such a rough start in life. But you've
certainly risen above it."

She smiled warily as he turned back to Lily, but the work
was a pleasant distraction, causing her to relax in Cole's company. All sensual tension vanished. She simply enjoyed being
with him and his horses. Soon they were laughing and talking easily.

"Would you like a cup of coffee before I drive you home?"
he asked after he secured Raider in his stall.

She wondered if he was merely being polite, but his gaze
was so intense, she couldn't resist.

"I'd love one," she lied, even though she never drank the
bitter stuff.

Side by side they walked down the road to his house in the
moonlight, each so wrapped up in their lighthearted banter
they failed to see the Lincoln parked in the shadows of the
huge live oak beside his house. He opened the front door as
they were laughing at a joke he'd made.

"John, is that you—at last?" His mother's biting tone cut
Maddie to the quick.

"Mother?"

"I was beginning to wonder if you'd ever come home."

"You should have called before coming if you don't like
being inconvenienced."

"I did call. Your phone was off, or you didn't bother to
answer."

Black silk rustled as his tall, elegantly slim mother stood
up. Her flawless features held no warmth. She kept her thin
nose high and angled away from Maddie.

"You should have let me know you were coming home,
dear," she said. "I would have had Angelica make dinner."

"I had other plans. You remember Maddie Gray, don' you?"

His mother's lips pursed as her icy stare flicked briefly to Maddie. "Vaguely," she lied in a voice that made Maddie feel small.

"Hello," Maddie said.

His mother's nose arched higher. "I'd prefer to talk to my son in private."

Feeling like a child unjustly put into time-out, Maddie nodded. Her first impulse was to leave, but she couldn't since Cole had driven her here. Then she remembered her letters. Maybe this was the perfect opportunity to search for them. "Cole, why don't I wait in your office?" Maddie said.

"Because the den is larger and much more comfortable," he replied.

"I'll be just fine in there. You and your mother should take the den." Before he could object, she hurried toward his office.

He followed her. "Why did you have to choose the messiest room in the house?" he whispered as she sank down in his big leather desk chair.

"Cole!" his mother snapped. "I said I've been waiting for over an hour!"

At his mother's command he frowned. "There are a few magazines on the desk. I won't be long," he said gently to Maddie.

When he closed the door, Maddie faced his messy desk. She wasn't happy that his mother despised her, but she refused to dwell on something she couldn't change. This might be her only chance to search for her letters.

Knowing that she probably didn't have much time, she leaned down and tugged at the bottom drawer. Just as she'd suspected, it was locked.

"Okay—so, I'll look through the top drawers first!" she whispered.

While she riffled through the other drawers, which was slow going because they were stuffed with so many papers, she heard raised voices.

Not wishing to eavesdrop, but not being able to stop herself, Maddie's ears pricked to attention even as she continued her rummaging.

"I know you've been lonely, dear. But this pathetic girl—Jesse Ray Gray's daughter, of all people?"

"You don't even know her."

"I know she probably came back here deliberately to flaunt herself the minute she heard Lizzie died."

Maddie gasped.

"Lizzie has been gone nearly a year."

"Well, the whole town's talking about Maddie skinny-dipping on our land this afternoon just to lure you."

Maddie's hands shook with such outrage she nearly slammed a drawer.

"You're wrong about everything, Mother."

When Maddie had searched all the drawers but the locked one, she angrily grabbed the keys she'd noticed earlier, lying on his desk.

"You're too gullible," his mother said. "This cheap girl has set her sights on you."

Cheap.... The word stung.

"Mother, your voice is too loud. She's my guest." He lowered his voice and must have persuaded his mother to do the same because Maddie couldn't hear them for a while.

Furiously, Maddie began trying different keys. Naturally, it was the last one that worked.

Suddenly the voices in the other room rose again.

"Mother, I have a question. Did Maddie try to call me six years ago before she left Yella? Did you talk to her?"

Maddie's heart began to beat very fast.

His mother didn't answer immediately. "Do you think I

can remember every call from six years ago? I can tell you one thing, though—*if* she'd called, you'd remember me giving you a piece of my mind."

"All right. Look, I need to take Maddie back to Miss Jennie's. Maybe you and I can have lunch before I go tomorrow."

A sob caught in Maddie's throat. She *had* to find her letters. She did not want his formidable mother threatening her or Noah, especially since Cole seemed to believe everything his mother said.

With unsteady fingers, Maddie sifted through the endless stack of deeds and contracts in the bottom drawer. When she heard footsteps approaching the office, she jumped back.

"Have you forgotten your manners completely?" his mother said. "Are you going to show me out or not?"

His heavy footsteps retreated. The front door opened and slammed shut.

If only his mother had insisted he walk her to her car. But she hadn't. Once again, Maddie heard his brisk footsteps heading toward his office.

In a panic, Maddie nudged the bottom drawer shut with her foot, only to let out a little cry when it jammed.

Grabbing a magazine, she whirled around in his chair and pretended to read an incomprehensible article about how irrigation affected hay yield.

"Sorry about that," he said in a world-weary tone from the doorway.

Maddie looked up. When she saw him glance at his keys, which were still dangling from the lock of his bottom drawer, her heart began to knock.

Then his concerned gaze refocused on her. "You're white as a sheet, and shaking, too."

Ashamed that the woman could still intimidate her, Maddie leaped up so that she could stand between him and the drawer. "I'm fine."

"I'm sorry you had to hear all that."

"I know she doesn't approve of me," Maddie said, hoping she sounded braver than she felt.

"Well, I think you're a wonderful person," he said.

"You do?"

"After what you told me? Of course!"

"You believed the worst of me when I left."

"Even that didn't stop me from caring about you."

Too bad he'd never made that fact known to her.

As he led her out of his office toward the kitchen, she thought he was being awfully nice even if he was a little more reserved after his mother's visit. He caught her hand in his and pressed it reassuringly in his larger palm. "Forget about her, okay?"

"She's right. The whole town's probably talking about me skinny-dipping to lure you by now."

"They're just jealous."

"Don't joke."

"Forget about her…and the town."

"Can you?"

"Look, she's my mother. I'm used to her trying to control every second of my life. I thought I'd learned how to handle her a long time ago, but then Lizzie died, and I went through a dark patch. Guilt, grief, regrets—I was pretty messed up. Mother wanted to move in with me, to take over. Fighting her helped snap me out of my funk. I know she loves me in her way, but I can't allow her to get too close. She's needy and critical."

"I'm sorry about Lizzie," she said again. "She was sweet. Even to me. She used to sneak down to the barn and watch me take care of the horses."

"Yes, she was sweet to everybody. But there's something I need to tell you. I didn't deserve her, and I'm not sure I made her happy. It's not always easy to be married to the town saint, you know."

Because he looked so troubled by this admission, and she thought he was going to say more, she didn't reply.

"She's gone," he said simply. "It's too late to change anything. Except there is one thing I can say for sure—she wouldn't mind you being here. She would have wanted me to see you and sort my feelings out. She loved me—in spite of the many ways I disappointed her."

He looked more at ease after he said that, less tense, and Maddie couldn't help but wonder if Lizzie had known all about Cole's desire for her and sensed his guilt. Maybe her sweet, forgiving nature had made him feel that he was a worse person than he really was.

But what did his marriage to Lizzie have to do with his feelings for Maddie now? Did he or did he not agree with his mother's low assessment of her? Could he ever respect her?

What if he could? What if he *did*?

Suddenly Maddie knew she couldn't leave; she couldn't return to Austin and marry Greg without finding out what Cole meant to her and what she meant to him. Greg was a good man. It would be unfair to risk hurting him as Cole believed he'd hurt Lizzie. She couldn't marry Greg until she came to terms with her feelings for Cole or purged him from her system.

"So—do you still feel like a cup of coffee?" he asked.

"I'm not much of a coffee drinker."

When his face darkened with disappointment, her own heart brimmed with wild, illogical joy.

He wants me to stay! Despite his mother's disapproval and the risk of more gossip!

No doubt his mother had come to warn them off each other. But Maddie was no longer a teenager who could be easily bullied. She had to know how Cole felt. His opinion mattered.

Not his mother's. It was time she stood up for herself, time she showed his mother and the gossips of Yella that she wasn't who they'd thought she was.

"I think I'd like a glass of wine," she said.

His brilliant smile made her tummy flip.

"White or red?"

She laughed, feeling warm and flushed from just looking at him. "You pick. What we drink is not my top priority tonight."

"Then what is?" An electric current charged the air between them. Looking charmingly baffled, he stared into her sparkling eyes.

"I can see I'll have to give you a great big hint." Because she simply couldn't resist, she reached up on her tiptoes and put both arms around his neck. When he made no move, she arched her body into his.

His black brows lifted quizzically, and for a few more seconds he hesitated. Then his strong hands at the back of her waist locked and pulled her closer. "You did say no touching," he whispered huskily.

"You know what they say about women being allowed to change their minds?"

His eyes blazed as he ran his knuckles up the gentle curve of her throat, causing her to shiver. Staring at her mouth, he cupped her chin, his thumb caressing the sensual fullness of her bottom lip. "I've been wanting to kiss you all night— and very badly." When she licked her lips, he groaned and snugged her against his hips more tightly. Without further invitation, his mouth came down on hers, hard. She opened her lips, sighing in soft pleasure when his tongue moved inside, probing the soft interior of her mouth so erotically he took her breath away.

Sensing her surrender, his pelvis crushed hers, communicating his blatant arousal.

"Oh, my," she said. "Is that for me?"

When she kissed him even more hungrily than before, he swung her up in his arms. "Baby, I can't believe you've finally come home...to me."

"I didn't intend to. But I'm kinda glad I did."

"Just kinda?"

"Way more than kinda," she whispered, nuzzling her cheek against his.

Still kissing her, he carried her to the kitchen where he grabbed a bottle of wine and a can of tonic water, his drink of choice ever since he'd pulled himself out of the booze hole he'd fallen into after Lizzie's death. Holding Maddie tightly, he mounted the stairs, taking them easily. Then he strode down the darkened hall toward his vast bedroom.

Laughing, feeling like a bride, she reached out and twisted the doorknob and pushed the door ajar for him.

"If you're going to say no again, say it now," he whispered in a low, urgent tone.

"I want you," she said. "And I'm weak. I've always been weak where you're concerned. But then, what do you expect from the bad girl of Yella, Texas?"

"I expect wild, wanton sex," he murmured as he kicked the bedroom door shut. "Lots of it."

Seven

She was lying under Cole in his dark bedroom writhing against his hot, hard, naked length. She was in his arms again after six years of abstinence, and he was doing all the wickedly delicious things she'd dreamed of for years. He was skimming his fingers over her everywhere, loving her with his lips and his exploring tongue.

Then, in the next moment, the horror of the past intruded on the sweetness of their fragile present.

She was a frightened, young girl again, trapped beneath another man, a vicious man she hated, whose rough hands and foul-smelling mouth tore at her body.

Suddenly, all the dark memories she'd worked so hard to suppress overpowered her.

With her hair still damp from a final afternoon swim and her heart full of love for Cole, she'd rushed home to the trailer fresh from having made love to him on the grassy bank beside the pool. Thinking herself alone, she'd let herself in, only to find her mother's boyfriend, Vernon, sprawled on the sofa in dirty, ripped jeans and a T-shirt. With his huge, tattooed arms, he'd seemed like a spider waiting for her in that tangled web of darkness as he'd squashed out his cigarette.

He'd come on to her before, and she was usually able to avoid being alone with him. "Why aren't you at work?" she'd asked.

An ugly, drunken snarl had distorted his scarred face as he lunged toward her. "What's it to you if I got fired? Bet I know who you've been with. The whole town knows about Prince Coleman Charming." When she'd tried to squeeze out the door again, he'd grabbed her arm, wrenching it behind her and dragging her back inside, locking the door.

"I know where you spend your time. You won't let me touch you because I'm not good enough. Then you chase Coleman like a bitch in heat. Who do you think you are, girl? Well, I'll tell you! You're Jesse Ray's girl, that's who! You're nobody! Worse! You're trailer trash, just like me! Hell, you're lucky to get me!"

Vernon had reeked of beer and cigarettes and worse as he'd slammed her against the wall and pressed his pelvis against her as she'd fought desperately to escape. How she'd reeked of those things, too, later, when he'd finished with her.

Afterward she'd felt so dirty and scared and ashamed. Most of all she'd felt powerless. Sore and battered, she'd cried and cried, but what good had her tears been? Vernon had laughed and said nobody would believe her if she ratted on him, not even her mother. And he'd been right.

When her mother had thrown them both out, Maddie had known she couldn't tell the authorities. If her mother hadn't believed her, there was no way the cold-eyed sheriff would. Nor would anyone else. Hadn't they always thought the worst of her?

Even before Vernon had hurt her, she'd always been afraid

Cole thought he was too good for her. Still, she'd gathered her courage and called him. Only that was when his mother had answered. In Maddie's broken emotional state, Mrs. Coleman's harsh words had compounded Vernon's injuries tenfold. She had crushed Maddie's spirit and her sweetest hope of love and happiness.

Don't think about the past! Don't!

Cole shifted his weight beside her, staring at her in the dark. Gently, his hands brushed her cheeks. "Your eyes are glassy and wild, and you're shivering and crying. Why?"

"Am I?" In shock, she traced her cheeks with her fingertips and realized they were wet. Thinking about Vernon could do this to her.

"No reason," she lied. All the secrets that had driven her from Yella still lay like a stone on her heart.

Cole drew her closer and bent his head to nuzzle her hair. "I've dreamed of this," he whispered. "All through my marriage to Lizzie, you were there between us. I wanted you even then. And I felt horrible about it."

"I know. I'm sorry," she said, empathizing more than was wise. His breath against her ear made her tremble.

"I felt so guilty. But I would lie in bed, with her beside me, thinking about you—about your lips, about how your nipples used to peak when I kissed them, about your silky black hair and how I loved to play with it. I think I hated you for that... more even than I hated you for Vernon."

At the mention of Vernon, Maddie sobbed hoarsely. "You don't know what you're saying. Or what happened. You don't know anything."

"Because you ran away with Vernon without ever telling me anything. So all I had to go on was what your mother said."

After his mother had been so cruel and Maddie had run from Yella, she hadn't let herself think about Cole because it had been too painful. Then she'd been afraid she was pregnant with Vernon's child. It was only when she'd realized how much Noah looked like Cole that she'd worked up the nerve to call him, but he'd hung up on her. So, she'd had to write it all down in those letters he hadn't bothered to read.

"I don't care about Vernon anymore," he said.

"You don't?"

"That was six years ago. You were young. I was your first. Maybe I was coming on too strong. Maybe you had to get away and be on your own to grow up. I only know that your coming back here is the best thing that's ever happened to me," he said. "I like who you seem to be now, and I don't want to ruin our reunion by blaming you for what's past. Don't cry. Please. Because I can't bear it if you do."

He kissed her brow and then her temples with warm lips that soothed. He'd always been so nice to her when they'd been lovers. While growing up, she'd hated feeling that she was condemned for her mother's sins. In his arms, she'd found an escape. Cole had made her feel as though she could change her life—before Vernon's vicious act had nearly destroyed her.

Cole seemed as wonderful tonight as he'd been that long-ago summer. His gentle voice and kind words made her swallow her salty tears. Hadn't Vernon ruined enough of her life? Because of him, she'd been afraid. She'd kept to herself and lived an impossibly lonely life until she'd met Greg.

"I won't cry," she said, rubbing her eyes with the backs of her hands. "My tears are all gone. See? So kiss me. Love me. Please, just love me again."

She needed new memories, beautiful memories with Cole, to make the bad ones lose their power.

"All right." He kissed her, but tenderly, sweetly, undemanding. His lips fell onto her brow, onto the pert tip of her upturned nose and then lightly onto her lips. Running his tongue over her breasts, he caressed her nipples with his hands while he held her close, slowly persuading her to put aside the past and all the pain and shame Vernon had inflicted on her for the pleasure that Cole alone could give her.

Soon his touches and kisses had her so dizzy with desire she forgot everything except her need to be with him. When he finally put on a condom and slid into her, she wrapped her arms and legs around him, moaning, clinging, so that he could sink deeper—oh, so much deeper—before he rode her. Then she clung to him and wept, but this time her tears came from joy...and the rush of new hope.

When his passion made him drive into her harder, his need to claim her primitive and demanding, she reveled in it, bracing herself for the power of his thrusts, for the pleasure of them, arching her hips to meet them, needing this forceful mating as much as he did. She circled his strong shoulders with her arms and surrendered with a completeness that stunned her, that wiped her clean of everything but her fierce desire to belong to him.

When finally he shuddered as he found his release, he cried out her name as if she were everything to him, and the sound of it made her sizzle and come in a blazingly glorious explosion of her own. For a long time after that, she held on to him, their hands locked, their damp brows touching. After six lonely years she wanted to prolong the moment of togetherness. Even when he pulled away, she murmured, clinging to him. Only in his arms and in his all-consuming passion had the dark shadow of Vernon briefly vanished.

Not that Cole seemed to mind her clinginess. No, he held her tightly and brushed his fingers through her hair, murmuring that she smelled of flowers and of her.

"You're so sweet. You're everything to me," he whispered. "Everything.... You always were. I don't care who your mother was or what my mother thinks. Those things don't matter."

Drowsily she lay in his arms, content, feeling utterly complete and happier than she'd felt in years.

He pulled her closer. For the first time in ages she wasn't afraid as she closed her eyes. Though she wasn't ready to contemplate telling him about Noah, she knew that tonight, if she woke up screaming as she sometimes did, he'd be there. What a wonderful feeling of security it was to know that.

When they awoke, he made love to her again. Afterward she felt an even greater sense of belonging only to him. The feeling wasn't based on anything more than the sensual pleasure of sex. But each time he made love to her, she felt happier, if that were possible. She snuggled closer against his warmth because he made her feel safe. Wrapped in his arms, she fell asleep.

Hours later, when she came awake with a start as she often did after one of her nightmares, Cole's strong arms no longer held her. As always, she'd been running from some unknown black terror. Just when she was nearly to safety, a strong male hand reached out of the darkness and pulled her down roughly. No matter how hard she fought the faceless figure, she couldn't free herself. Trapped and helpless underneath him, she opened her eyes.

Only the monster wasn't there. He never was. She was all alone in the hot darkness of Cole's bedroom, drenched with perspiration from her nightmare. Her fingers played across the nightstand searching for her flashlight, but it wasn't there. Then she remembered she was at Cole's, not in her own room where she kept a flashlight by the bed. But she did have a small one in her purse, which she'd left on that little table downstairs near the front door.

"Cole?" she whispered in a panic. "Cole!"

When he didn't answer, she moved toward his side of the bed. If only he would wake up and take her in his arms, she wouldn't feel afraid. But his side of the bed was empty. She pushed free of the cool tangles of sheets and sat up in the dark.

Shakily, she grabbed his pillow, which was cool although it held his scent, and pressed it against her lips. Because of her nightmare, all the newfound confidence Cole's lovemaking had instilled in her deserted her.

Where was he? Why had he left? He'd made her feel so safe and cherished, but was their night together just rebound sex for him after losing Lizzie?

Desolation swamped her. The distrustful mindset she'd experienced ever since Vernon's attack slid back into place. Suddenly she was filled with doubts about everything. About her feelings, about having given herself with such abandon to Cole when she barely knew the man he now was or what his true intentions toward her might be.

Did he believe what his mother had said, that Maddie was as low as ever and after him for his money? Did he regret sleeping with her? Or was she just a sexual outlet? Would she never be free of the stigma of her childhood in his eyes?

Made more anxious by her nightmare, she felt increasingly disconcerted by his absence as she stared at the flickering shadows on the ceiling. When he didn't return after a lengthy interval, her doubts built to a terrifying level. She grabbed a sheet and pulled it around herself. Determined to reassure him that he owed her nothing, she stood up and padded out of the room to search for him in his vast, shadowy house.

When Cole switched on the overhead lamp in his office, his gaze zeroed in on the keys dangling from the lock of his bottom drawer.

"Son of a…" Cole cursed vividly under his breath. He would never have left his keys there. He remembered Maddie's look of alarm when he'd entered the office earlier in the evening. She'd been pale, and her hands had shaken as she'd read that boring magazine article he hadn't been able to get through about hay. He'd thought she was upset because of the hateful things his mother had said. Now he wondered.

Had Maddie played him?

The vague impression that something was not quite right in his office had niggled worrisomely at the back of his mind even after he'd collected Maddie, but he'd been so focused on trying to make up to her for his mother's rudeness that he'd dismissed any suspicions he might have had.

Then they'd slept together, and their hot sex had distracted him further. Had she intended that? When he'd awakened, as he often did in the middle of the night, and had begun to ruminate on the various ongoing challenges in his life, he'd replayed in his mind Juan's message concerning the driller who'd failed to show after cashing the advance check. Since Cole couldn't do anything about the driller until morning, he'd decided to come down to his office to see what could be done.

Now he remembered thinking there had been something furtive in Maddie's manner after his mother had left. He remembered that she'd insisted on waiting in his office even when he'd tried to talk her out of it.

More suspicious than ever, Cole knelt and touched the keys. Then he yanked the drawer open wider. He'd intended to read the letters the first chance he had after Maddie had mentioned them. They'd been on his mind when he'd gotten home with Raider, but Juan had called. After that, Joe had wanted to discuss what the vet had to say about a sick bull. Then the roofer who hadn't shown up to reroof the barn had called with a litany of excuses. Cole had hung up from that call furious. One thing had led to another, and he hadn't thought of the letters again until he'd been driving back to Miss Jennie's to pick up Maddie.

Had Maddie chosen to wait in his office so she could search for her letters?

What the hell was in those damn letters anyway?

Curious now, he grabbed the piles of deeds and mortgages he stored in the fireproof lower drawer and tossed them carelessly onto the floor. Then he riffled through the remaining documents until he got to the bottom, where he found the two yellowed envelopes exactly where he'd placed them five years ago. Exactly where Lizzie must have dutifully replaced them.

Whistling, he sank back into his chair and held them up so he could study the postmarks. Then he grabbed his bronze letter opener and ripped into the first letter. After the first sentence, he sat forward, his heart thudding with a vengeance.

When I left Yella, I was pregnant.

Pregnant. He whistled again. He knew the kid was Vernon's. Why should the word slam him? It was the way she put it somehow, right in the beginning of a letter she'd addressed to *him*.

Her mother had a reputation for getting her lovers to pay for stuff. Had Maddie been trying to stick him with Vernon's kid?

Not that I realized I was pregnant that final day in Yella. And later, I admit I thought the baby had to be Vernon's since you were always so careful to protect me.

Anger ate through him like acid at her admission that she'd slept with Vernon. Which was ridiculous, since her mother had told everybody Maddie had run off with Turner years ago.

But Noah has your dark hair and green eyes and your widow's peak…. And he is like you, Cole. He collects arrowheads just like you did as a little boy. He is just so bone-deep good, in all the ways a person, even a little, mischievous person, can be good. He's so good,

Cole, that I know now he's yours. You're welcome to do a DNA screening of course.

Noah? His? Good?

Through his shock, Cole felt her gladness in that final word. Obviously, she'd seen through Turner even back then. But she'd slept with the nasty creep anyway; she'd thought she was pregnant by him. For more than a year of Noah's life, she'd believed Vernon to be the father, so she hadn't told Cole when he'd been free and able to claim his son.

Cole thought he'd forgiven her for leaving with Turner, but there was a roar in his ears. Tonight, when Cole had made her his again, he'd wanted to erase their past, to erase Turner, to forgive all. But the letter made the past and all its pain feel fresh again, made him hot at the thought of her ever having been with that man, even for one night.

Unable to forget her sweetness and her total surrender in his bed a few hours earlier, Cole clenched his fist, seething as he fought for control.

What did his anger matter, if she was right about Noah being his son?

Cole thought of all her struggles and achievements. No matter what she'd done, if she was right about Noah being his, she was the mother of his son.

Cole's big hands shook as he slashed into her second letter.

I know you received my first letter because you signed for it, and if I don't hear from you after this one, I'll know for sure that you want nothing to do with Noah— or me—ever again. I understand why you would feel that way, and I promise, you don't need to worry that I'll hound you any further. If I don't hear from you in two weeks, I will consider you free of all obligations toward our son and me, and I'll go on with my life.

Cole sank back in his chair and buried his face in his hands as he remembered how coldly he'd rejected her over the phone, how coldly he'd tossed her letters into his bottom drawer.

Free? She'd really believed he would knowingly cast his son aside! How could she have ever believed that of him?

But...he had signed for the letters. And he hadn't answered her. Was it really fair to blame her for drawing that conclusion when he'd drawn his own hellish conclusions about her?

How had she raised their son alone? With no money? While struggling to educate herself?

Worst of all, what had Noah done without because of his father's blind arrogance? At the very least, Noah had never known he had a father who would have cared about him.

Cole knew too well how such a revelation could tear up lives. His own father had had a secret son by his first love, Marilyn. That son was his older brother, Adam. Neither Marilyn nor his dad had known she was pregnant when they'd broken up. By the time she'd found out, his father had been in the military overseas. When she'd finally located him, he'd already married Cole's mother. Although his father hadn't openly claimed Adam, he'd assumed full responsibility and had secretly supported Marilyn and Adam. He'd even gone to see them as often as he could. It wasn't until Cole's dad was gray-faced on his deathbed that he'd confessed everything to Cole and had begged him to go and see Adam in West Texas.

"I always felt I had to protect your mother from knowing about Marilyn and Adam. You know how she is, so fine and proper...and so unyielding and self-righteous. For her sake, I never told you about your brother. I want you to go to him now. Try...to be a brother to him. And please ask your mother to forgive me."

Cole had asked her, all right, but his mother was still very bitter about Adam. Against her wishes, Cole had taken Adam into the family business as his father had wished. They'd even become close, considering they hadn't grown up together and still didn't totally trust each other.

Cole's hand dug into his scalp as recriminating emotions tore at him.

Damn it, you thought you were protecting your marriage and Lizzie when you refused to take Maddie's calls or read her letters.

No, you were a selfish, arrogant coward...just like your father.

That's not true! Dad did the best he could.

What is your own arrogance compared to Maddie running off with Turner?

Forget Turner. Forget what she did. You have a son—Noah. He has to come first.

Eight

Cole got up and turned off the light. Unable to face returning to the bed where Maddie slept when he didn't know if her warmth and sweetness were real, he remained in his dark office and shut his eyes.

What was the truth?

Were the people in Yella right about her after all?

Unsavory as the subject was, Cole had to dig the whole story out of her. Why the hell had she run away with Turner? Why did she turn white and look scared every time his name was mentioned? Had her mother lied?

Not that the answers to any of those questions mattered nearly as much as Noah.

What the hell was he going to do? How would he ever make up for six lost years?

Cole must have fallen asleep because he jumped when he heard a soft footfall in the den. When a woman's slim hand pushed the door ajar, and the narrow beam of a tiny flashlight fell on his dangling keys, he froze.

Where the hell had she gotten a flashlight?

Swiftly, Maddie, who was swathed in white from head to toe, entered the office and knelt beside the drawer. She'd been as silent as a ghost until she found the drawer open... and empty. Then she let out a strangled scream.

He snapped on the lamp beside him with a hard jerk of his wrist. "Looking for these?"

When he held up her letters, her slanting eyes widened. Then she dropped her flashlight and it rolled under his desk.

"Give them to me," she whispered, her exotic face going even whiter as she leaned down to retrieve her flashlight.

"Sure!" When he laid them on his desk, she snatched them away. "Why not? I already read them," he said.

"You had no right."

"Really? You claim we have a son together, and I have no right? Tell me something. Did you come over here today just to get these letters? When you failed to find them while my mother was here, did you stay and sleep with me just so you could stay a little longer and sneak back down here and try to get these letters?"

"You can believe that if you want to. You've believed worse of me."

His dark eyes were probably as lethally fierce as he felt, because she quickly averted her gaze.

"I wonder why?" he asked, hating it when she paled further. "I want the truth this time, damn it."

"No, you don't. Nobody in this town has ever wanted that from me. All of you want to despise me. So go ahead! I should be used to it by now." But her eyes were wild and her voice caught on a raw sob.

"I want to know if my mother's right, if you used your beauty to play me for a fool! And I want to know if you used your beauty when we were kids. Did you chase me because you thought I was rich and you'd be bettering yourself? You are, obviously, by your own admission, ambitious."

"I never chased you, if you'll remember! You chased *me*. And then…when I realized you'd never really wanted me for more than sex, I walked away."

"With Vernon?" he snarled.

She gasped. "I let you go." She paused. "But yes, I am ambitious. Yes, I want to give my child a better start in life than I had back then. And not only my child…but to give other children a better start. I don't want any child to have to grow up like I did!"

Something earnest and heartbroken in her eyes tore at him, but he ignored it.

"Right—you're the saint now, and I'm some entitled, arrogant demon from hell who got you pregnant and then callously rejected you and our son after I married another woman!"

Despite her stricken expression, she notched her chin a fraction of an inch higher.

"All I know is that tonight…coming here…what we did… was a mistake," she whispered. "I should never have confided in you at the pool, or slept with you."

"Well, you did, damn it!"

"Can't we just please forget tonight ever happened?"

He stared at her pale, forlorn face in disbelief. *No!* he wanted to yell.

Forget he had a son? Forget how seeing her again, how having her in his arms again, had made him feel so complete and so connected to her on a soul-deep level that his loneliness of six years had fallen away? Forget that despite everything he knew about her and everything people said about her, she looked defenseless and stricken and so damn innocent he wanted to take care of her? Forget he'd begun to trust her again and she'd disappointed him? Hell, furious as he was, she had him crazy with desire. How could he feel this way about her even now, when he'd just learned they had a son she'd planned to conceal from him forever?

She was as unscrupulous and selfish as her mother, but, on some level, he didn't care.

Why the hell did his heart and body refuse to believe what his mind knew about her? Fool that he was, he still wanted her.

Not that he was about to let on how much power she had over him.

"Once I would have given anything to hear you say you wanted Noah, anything.... I couldn't believe it when your only response was my two self-addressed, green postcards that came back with your boldly scrawled signature. After that there was nothing. No phone call. No letter. No email. Nothing. I kept waiting to hear from you. I went through hell. So, no—I don't care how you feel now because I can't trust you. Don't you see? I can't let myself care. I'm a mother. I have to do what's best for Noah."

"Right," he growled. "You're the trustworthy one. You were going to keep your son from ever knowing his real father. How do you think he'd feel about that if he ever found out?"

Clutching her letters against her breasts, which were covered by a long sheet, she squared her shoulders and backed toward the door. "I'm going to get dressed. I want you to drive me back to Miss Jennie's."

The finality in her tone cut him like a blade. But he refused to react, refused to let her see how her indifference shredded him.

"Sure. But we talk tomorrow. Don't you dare even think about leaving Yella before we talk. Because if you do, I'll make things worse for you. I could come to Austin, meet the do-gooders who pay you, tell them what people here think about you."

"Why would you do that?"

"Noah is my son, too."

"Why are you doing this? Surely you can't want Noah!" she whispered.

"Wrong!" He sprang to his feet, truly infuriated now. "I didn't know about him! Now that I do, you're going to have to deal with it, the same as I am! I could do a lot for Noah, you know. And for you."

"I want you out of my life!"

Heat engulfed him.

Her words pushed him over some dangerous edge, because he wanted her in his life as much as he wanted Noah. Even now, knowing that she'd probably slept with him for the sole purpose of remaining in his house long enough to get her letters so he would never find out about Noah, he wanted her.

"Well, that's too damn bad! Noah has two parents!"

After she'd left him for Vernon, he'd felt dead. Even when he'd been married to Lizzie, he'd felt dead. For years, he'd buried himself in his work in an attempt to forget her. Lizzie had felt neglected, and rightfully so. When Lizzie had died, he'd chosen booze so he wouldn't have to face the guilt and the emptiness that ravaged him—or the insane need he'd felt to search for Maddie.

When he'd seen her at the pool this morning, the sun had seemed to brighten and the water to sparkle with a special blinding radiance. Because of her, the whole world had seemed new and fresh. He couldn't tell her any of that, though, because then she'd know her power and use it against him.

"I don't like this any better than you do!" he yelled as she ran out of the room and up the stairs with his sheet trailing behind her.

Angry as he was, the knowledge that her voluptuous body was soft and naked under his sheet had him brick-hard again.

When he tore after her, he intended to appease her at least a little before pulling her into his arms, but she turned on him at the top of the stairs. And the words she flung at him through her sobs slammed him like mortal blows.

"I'm engaged to be married! To a wonderful man, I'll have you know! He grew up poor like me, so he understands me. He's a teacher, so he's wonderful with kids. He would never reject and abandon me, the way you did, and he already considers Noah his son. He's everything that Noah needs in a father."

"Then why the hell did you just sleep with me?" he thundered.

"Hormones. It was a horrible mistake. Please, just drive me home, and stay out of our lives!"

"You ask the impossible," he whispered in a ravaged tone. "Where's his damn ring anyway?"

"We're...we're informally engaged."

She raced into his bedroom and slammed the door.

Moonlight flooded his bedroom as Maddie sank down on his big bed with its tumbled sheets where they'd made love such a short time ago, where she'd been so happy...so foolishly happy, she thought now.

When she'd awakened from her nightmare filled with doubts and insecurities, he hadn't been there, and she'd felt rejected and afraid of her own powerful emotions.

She'd felt afraid that he didn't care about her, that he never had and that he never could. She thought maybe to him she was just a carnal pleasure—and of no more consequence than a coveted toy a spoiled child might enjoy from time to time.

Had Cole come after her when Vernon had hurt her? Had Cole rescued her like a knight in shining armor? Not that she believed in fairy tales, but still... Had he even questioned her mother's sordid story? Or had he simply believed the worst, like everybody else? Had he ever tried to find her? Or had he already been chasing after Lizzie—a proper girl, Yella's sweetheart? If she'd mattered to him at all, if she'd had a background he'd approved of, wouldn't he have found a way to reach her?

All her old doubts and insecurities had torn at her as she'd lain in the dark. Then she'd gotten up the nerve to search for him to determine his true feelings.

The lower part of the house had been dark when she'd made it down the stairs, so she'd made her way to her purse on the little table by the window and pulled out her tiny flashlight, which she always carried.

Thinking maybe he'd fallen asleep on a sofa, she hadn't wanted to turn on the lights as she searched for him.

When she hadn't found him on any of his big sofas or easy chairs, she'd seen his office door ajar. The lower drawer had been open, and she'd let out a little scream after she'd sunk to her knees and realized he'd probably read her letters.

At the realization that he knew about Noah, that the knowledge was why he hadn't come back to bed, she'd felt confused and scared, crazy. She hadn't been ready to face him, to talk to him about Noah. No, she'd felt too vulnerable after the sex—sex that had revealed how much she still cared for him. So when she'd found herself suddenly backed into a corner about Noah, she'd reacted to Cole's righteous anger and accusations defensively. By becoming furious, she'd made a royal mess of everything.

But she wasn't about to let hot sex weaken her into agreeing to include him in her son's life when that might not be the best thing for her and Noah. Cole hadn't been there when she'd needed him the most—when she'd been scared and helpless.

Well, maybe she and Noah didn't need him now.

What the hell was she doing up there? Sulking? Plotting? Or just feeling as sick at heart and confused as he was?

With a heavy heart, Cole mounted the stairs and waited outside that closed door until Maddie dressed. When she came out, she rushed past him and down the stairs without looking at him or speaking to him. On the way downstairs he found a tiny red flashlight on a carpeted stair. He kneeled and closed his fist around it. Uttering a low animal sound, he jammed it in his pocket.

Neither of them spoke as his truck ripped through the suffocating darkness on their way to Miss Jennie's rambling house, but the atmosphere inside the cab felt as charged as one of his gas wells about to blow. When at last he slammed on the brakes in front of Miss Jennie's and the truck jerked to a standstill, he jumped out and raced around to open her door.

She stayed where she was. Then, without a word, she began rummaging in her purse.

"Looking for something?"

"My flashlight. I must have dropped it somewhere."

He yanked it out of his pocket and flashed the narrow beam inside her purse.

With a frown she flung herself out of the door and grabbed it from him. "I'm perfectly capable of seeing myself to the door," she snapped.

Turning her back on him, she aimed the tiny beam on the sidewalk and marched stiffly toward the porch.

She didn't give him so much as a backward glance as she let herself inside the dark house and bolted the door behind her. Miss Jennie wasn't one to keep her shades down, so he watched Maddie's flashlight bob as she made her way to the back, watched when her bedroom light went on. Then her door closed, and the front of the house was dark again.

"Baby, if you think this is finished, you're very wrong," he growled softly. "If Noah's mine, he's mine. Not Greg's. I'll use DNA and the whole damn legal system to get him."

Nine

Usually, challenges seemed less daunting to Cole the next morning. Not today. Too much was at stake.

As soon as the sun flamed like a red-hot ball of fire against a mauve horizon, Cole dragged himself out of bed and made coffee. Although he had a headache from hell and burned with impatience, he had called Juan about the well. Fortunately, the driller had just arrived, so Cole could vent some of his frustration by blasting that glib, overpaid shirker who thoroughly deserved it. After the call, he went for a run before he drove over to Miss Jennie's.

Morning doves cooed in the treetops above Miss Jennie's house. Shadows from her big oaks slanted across her overgrown lawn. The last traces of ground fog hovered at the fringes of the brush where his ranch bordered her property.

For a long moment Cole stayed in the cab of his truck and observed the single light burning in the kitchen window. Maybe Maddie hadn't been able to sleep very well. He knew *he* hadn't. No, after dropping Maddie off last night, he'd lain in his bed, tossing and turning, torturing himself with visions of her lying in her fiancé's arms.

Gathering his courage, he dragged himself out of the truck and walked up to the front door and knocked. He was about to raise his hand again when the door opened and Cinnamon wheeled around from the back porch, yapping.

Propped on crutches, Miss Jennie, whose wrinkled face was softened by her bright blue eyes, beamed up at him sweetly as Cinnamon rushed inside.

"Good mornin', Cole. I expect you're here to see my darlin' Maddie."

"You're right about that."

"Well, she's in the shower. The poor thing's as pale as a ghost this morning and seems plumb tuckered out. I don't think she slept much last night. I heard her pacing this morning, but you come on in...that is, if you don't mind waitin' for her."

He removed his Stetson. "I don't mind," he said politely, feeling ashamed of his own violent emotions as he stepped inside Miss Jennie's quiet, orderly parlor, which was filled with faded carpets, well-used antiques and the scarred piano that every kid in town had hammered on, including him.

"I have a fresh pot of coffee in the kitchen. Or if you'd prefer a soda, there's several in the fridge. I think I'd like a soda myself. Maybe you could open one for me, and we could chat at the kitchen table while we wait for our girl. Or sit on the screened porch."

"Wherever it's cooler."

"That would be the kitchen. I've got the air on."

Cole poured himself a mug of coffee and set a chilled can of soda before Miss Jennie, who was quick to thank him.

"I can't manage these crutches and get a soda out of the fridge at the same time," she said. "Not enough hands. Maddie's been so good to come here and help me with little things like that. She's fed Cinnamon and chased him, watered the plants and done the laundry. Mainly, though, we've caught up on our visitin'. I'm mighty proud of how she turned out."

He nodded courteously. He had immense respect for Miss Jennie, who had been his senior English teacher as well as Maddie's, only Miss Jennie hadn't championed him. Quite the opposite. Once, when his grades had fallen, she'd kept him from playing football for six weeks even though his parents and the coaches had pressured her to relent.

"I never knew you were friends with Maddie back when she lived here, you being a Coleman and all. She never once mentioned you until that awful night when she came here and said she had to leave Yella for good. She told me plenty about you that night, though. Cried her heart out, she did, poor thing, because you were so high-and-mighty, so far out of her reach. I told her to call you and lay it all out—to give you a chance. But that only made her weep harder because she said she already had and that you'd made it clear you thought she was trash and didn't want her."

Cole clenched his hands into fists and then unclenched them.

"There was nothing I could say to cheer her after that. She just said, 'He doesn't want me. He never will. I'm scared. You've got to help me get out of this town, or I'll end up just like my mother.' So I did."

Whatever else Maddie might have been that night, he now knew she'd been scared, and he hadn't been there for her. He was going to find out what the hell had happened to her that had made her run. It might take a while, peeling through the layers of the truth, but he was determined. First, though, he had to deal with Noah.

"She turned out real nice, didn't she?" Miss Jennie's blue eyes drilled into him.

"She did turn out nice," he muttered, feeling defensive.

"Miss Jennie!" Maddie stood in the doorway. Her stern voice and her ashen face were enough to make Miss Jennie swallow whatever she'd been about to confide.

"Hello, Cole," Maddie said stonily.

He stood up awkwardly, having forgotten all he'd intended to say to her after Miss Jennie's startling revelation.

It didn't make sense that Maddie had come to see Miss Jennie, of all people, on the night she'd been so mad with love she'd supposedly run off with Vernon. And Miss Jennie had confirmed what Maddie had told him about having tried to call him. What did it mean that she'd been crying her heart out because of *him,* and yet she'd still left with Vernon?

"We have to talk," he muttered gloomily.

"I don't have long," Maddie said in a crisp tone. "Miss Jennie needs me."

"I'll be fine right here with my soda and my morning paper. You two take Cinnamon out into the back garden and talk. There's some shade, so it's not too hot at this hour with the breeze. But mind that you make Cinnamon leave Bessie's chickens alone, so George, her husband, doesn't take a notion to shoot him again. You take all the time you need. I'll be just fine in here."

Tension throbbed through Cole as he pushed the screen door open and called to Cinnamon. The dog wheeled between their legs, barking. Then, of course, the dog rushed straight for Bessie's chicken coop.

"I hope George doesn't take aim at Cinnamon and shoot you or me by mistake," Cole said to lighten the mood. "He's a lousy shot."

A tight-lipped Maddie whirled on him as soon as they were where Miss Jennie could neither see nor hear them. "We have nothing to say to each other!"

"Why don't we start with the fact that I've had a son I

haven't known about for six damn years." Deliberately, he kept his tone soft.

When she shut her eyes, he was sure it was to block him out, not because the sun slanting through the oaks was so brilliant.

"I want to see him," Cole said. "To know him. For him to know me. As soon as it can be arranged and you feel that Noah is prepared, I want to meet him. Is that so wrong?"

"This has all happened so fast, I can't think. All I know is that you weren't there when we needed you. We've built a life—apart from you. It wasn't easy, I'll admit. I know you said you could do a lot for Noah, but the man I'm going to marry, Greg, can take care of us. He'll work hard to make us happy."

"Noah's still my son," Cole said. "I want to meet this *other* man, who's going to have a big part in Noah's life."

Out of the corner of his eye, Cole saw Bessie's shade lift.

"Please, if you ever felt anything for me…just go on with your own life. I was doing just fine without you."

"Well, maybe I wasn't doing just fine—not even before I knew about Noah. Maybe I want some answers. For six damn years I believed you jilted me and ran off with Vernon. In your letters that I stupidly didn't open, you said that you believed Noah was Vernon's. You sounded glad that he wasn't, like you were glad to think I might be Noah's father. Why? Miss Jennie just told me that you came to her right before you left Yella."

"Miss Jennie shouldn't be talking to you."

"Well, she called it an awful night. She said you told her about us, that you were crying and that you were in some kind of trouble. If that's true, I hope you'll trust me enough someday to tell me what happened."

"It's too late." Her flat voice was so faint he could barely hear her.

"Why did you tell her all about me if you were going to run off with Vernon? What the hell really happened that night?"

Her eyes grew huge and filled with pain. "I'm going to marry Greg, so none of this matters."

"We have a son. I want to know what happened."

"I can't go back there."

"I'm not asking you to go back. I'm asking you to communicate...honestly."

Refusing to look at him, she bit her bottom lip.

"Why did you sleep with me yesterday?"

"Because I'm weak and cheap...like my mother."

Was she? Grimly, he studied her wan face. He wished she could trust him enough to level with him.

Feeling so frustrated he wanted to shake her, he balled his fists and slid them into his pockets. "Maybe I would have been fool enough to buy that story before yesterday, but not now. I think you ran away from Yella because something terrible happened to you. I think you were scared and helpless, and I wasn't there for you. I think the woman who put herself through college while she raised my son alone, the woman who has a decent job now and a schoolteacher fiancé who's reputedly a damned paragon—that woman is the last thing from weak and cheap. I want the truth!"

She caught her breath. "Okay...like I keep telling you, the truth is that last night—the sex, I mean—was a mistake that I deeply regret."

"Not for me, it wasn't! It's the first good, completely honest thing that's happened to me in six years!"

It was bad timing that he'd read her letters right after that and had been forced to confront her about Noah. It would have been so much better for both of them if they'd had time to grow their relationship before they'd gotten into anything so heavy. But here he was—in too deep—with a woman he wasn't sure of. It was either sink or swim. He, for one, was determined to swim.

"I can't believe that," she began. "You're a Coleman, and I'm Jesse Ray's no-good daughter."

"Will you stop using the way everybody abused you as a weapon to club me? You've always been way more than that, and you know it."

Hardly knowing what he intended, he spanned the distance that separated them. So what if Bessie's shade notched up another inch or two. Wrapping Maddie, who smelled of shampoo and soap and her own sweet self, in his arms, he pulled her close.

"Even though you don't want me right now, you feel perfect in my arms."

When she tried to push free, he tightened his grip. Freeing her hands, he slid his arms around her waist.

"Cole, don't make this more difficult than it has to be."

"Kiss me," he begged. "You're going to have to prove to me you regret the sex." He paused. "I now believe you tried to call me the night you ran away. I believe my mother said something terrible that hurt you very deeply when you were already upset and terrified. I don't know why she doesn't want to admit it. I can only imagine she sensed the depth of my feelings for you and was too scared to confront me because she was afraid I'd choose you. No doubt she thinks she was acting in my best interests. Baby, I want you to trust me enough to tell me what happened that night."

"It's too awful."

"Maybe it will be easier to bear if you tell me."

Her lovely face crumpled. "I don't think so."

"I let you down. Okay. I know. I'm so sorry," he whispered.

"I don't know who you'll really believe—me or the gossips."

"If you'd talk to me, it would give me more ammunition against the gossips, wouldn't it?"

When she sighed, he hoped that maybe he was getting through to her.

"I'm such a fool," she murmured as she laid her head upon his chest. "I always was where you were concerned. I shouldn't listen to anything you ever say...especially when you hold me. I can't think."

"I was the fool. I never should have married Lizzie just because you'd run off and my dad was dead and my mother was hounding me all the time about Adam. I should have left Yella, left them all, and tried to find you."

"Maybe it would have just made things worse. By then, I knew I was pregnant. My life was such a mess. I was needy and desperate and struggling to find myself and carve out a new life. I wouldn't be who I am now if anything had been different. But all that's over and done with."

Stroking her hair, he held her. "I hate it that you had to face all that alone. I'm here now, and what I want is for you to marry me instead of Greg."

"What? You don't know what you're saying. That's impossible."

"Why? Noah's my son."

"But you're a Coleman, and I'm who I am. Marriage would mean we'd have to make a life together. We've been apart for six years, so we don't even really know each other at this point. You had a three-month secret affair with a girl who was forbidden, and we had yesterday. What else do we have?"

"Noah. Last night. Chemistry."

She blushed. "My mother ruined her life because her libido led her to make so many terrible choices. And there's your mother, who hates me."

"She'll either change her mind, or she won't see much of me or her grandson."

"There's Noah and how his grandmother's condemnation of me might damage him. I don't want what she and other people here think about me to make him see me as cheap."

"He wouldn't."

"Other children, other people, can be so cruel. You don't know, since you never suffered the kind of cruelty I did while growing up here."

"I'd be giving him my name and my protection. That will count for a lot in the future, just as it counts for a lot to everybody in Yella."

"Other people would side with your mother, her friends, everyone in Yella, even Adam.... They'd make me feel like I used to feel. I want to forget the past—all of it."

"We don't have to live here. And you're wrong about Adam. He and I don't agree on a lot of things, but he likes you. When he told me how beautiful and classy you were, nothing could stop me from racing back to Yella."

"Really?"

"I was irresponsible as hell to leave my oil well. I came back solely to see you." He held her tightly. "I'm sorry about the past," he whispered.

Very gently, he leaned down and laved the back of her ear with his tongue, causing her to flush beguilingly.

"Stop! I can't think when you do that," she whispered, her voice soft and breathy. "And I have to think."

"No. You've been doing too much thinking. Feelings count, too, you know. I think we fell into bed last night because we both wanted each other so badly we couldn't resist."

"In my life, lust has been a destroyer."

Slowly his fingers tucked her hair behind her ear. "Okay. I'll admit to a tad of lust, but not to the destroying kind. I never got over you, Maddie Gray. Because I cared about you."

"I don't believe that."

"Only because, after what you've been through, you're

too afraid. I don't blame you. But if you'd only give me another chance—"

"You're just lonely…because of Lizzie."

"I was hellishly lonely after you left…even after I married Lizzie."

"You haven't had time to think this through. Don't you see that it would never work?" She brushed at her throat with her fingertips as if suddenly she was too hot. When she tried to remove his hand, he wove his fingers through hers and brought her knuckles against his warm lips, his gentle kisses causing her to shudder.

"We'll have to find a way to make it work," he said.

When she glanced up at him, her beautiful eyes were aglow with fear and a wild, desperate hope.

"Let me go!" she begged.

Lowering his head so fast she couldn't dodge his lips, he claimed the exquisite softness of her mouth. When his tongue slid inside, she rasped in a breath.

"You have to break up with Greg," Cole muttered hoarsely. "You have to know that such a marriage wouldn't stand a chance when it's me you really want…in bed anyway."

"I can't care about that."

"You must, if you marry him wanting me. I could tell you a thing or two about marrying for the wrong reasons. About trying to make the wrong relationship work."

"Your argument doesn't stand. You and I would be marrying for the wrong reasons. I had this perfect plan…."

"You don't think I had a few plans myself? Last night blew all our plans to bits."

"I won't be bullied into a loveless marriage."

"Put like that, my proposal stinks. But your assessment is inaccurate. We'd be marrying for love—for the mutual love of our son."

"You don't know him."

"He's mine. I want him to be legitimate. I'd think that would matter to you since your mother didn't marry your father and people looked down on you for it."

"Oh… You do play dirty." She stared at him, aghast.

"When I have to. It's very simple. Go back to Austin. Tell Greg about me. Say you're confused, that you need time. In the meantime, introduce me to Noah as a good friend of yours, so we can start preparing him to accept me as your husband and his father. Then slowly we'll sort this out…*together*."

"No."

"I want to give Noah a stable life," he said smoothly.

"Do you think I don't want that?"

"Good. We agree on the fundamentals. We both want what's best for our son, and we both want each other."

"You don't love me."

"You don't love me either, but I'm not whining about it. I'm asking you to marry me."

"You're impossible…arrogant…entitled…"

He smiled as he waited for her to finish cataloging his many faults.

"But I want to marry you. I want to take care of you. I want to make up for six years of neglecting you and my son. Surely that makes up for two or three of my sins."

"You don't love me," she repeated.

Maybe not, but no way was he letting her go again, not after last night. For better or worse, she was his. Just like Noah was his. She just didn't know it yet.

He didn't like it that she'd intended to keep him from ever finding out about Noah, and he didn't like that she'd planned to marry Greg, but he had to focus on what he wanted—Noah and her—if he was going to win her over to his point of view. He didn't want another man being a father to Noah now that Cole was free to marry and claim his son.

As he held her and stared down at her lovely face, his blood began to thrum as he remembered how she'd felt last night in his arms. Suddenly, he was tired of arguing. As always, he marveled that she could arouse him so easily, so quickly— and that he could do the same to her.

"Maybe I don't love you, but I like a lot of things about you. For one thing, you're too damn beautiful to argue with and you're making me unbearably hot," he said.

"What?"

"Since everybody already thinks you lured me to my pool to go skinny-dipping yesterday, why don't we go there now... and actually do it?"

Her luminous eyes went so dark and shot so many sparks at him, he was afraid she was about to pull back her hand and take a swing at him. When she didn't, when she simply stared at him with what became a charming, incredulous expression on her blushing face, he relaxed and grew even hotter for her.

"Now?" she demanded. "We're in the middle of an argument. You can't be serious!"

Relieved that she hadn't said no, his hands twisted in her hair. He pulled her head back and her body flush against his own so that she could feel his erection. She gasped and cast a frantic look toward Bessie's window.

"Feel what you do to me," he whispered, right before he kissed her long and passionately. "Believe me—I'm very serious."

"But we were arguing about getting married. You can't just switch gears—"

"Who's switching? Obviously, everything we do together turns me on, which proves how much fun marrying you would be."

"Bessie's probably watching," she murmured, struggling to free herself.

"So? If we're going to be talked about, Miss Gray, we might

as well give the old biddies an X-rated kiss or two to speculate about, don't you think?"

When he laughed, her lips quirked as she attempted to suppress her own smile. "Just because I can't stay mad at you doesn't mean I intend to marry you."

"I can't stay mad at you either, which I take as a good sign for two people considering marriage," he countered.

She smiled a little.

"Hey, do you have a picture of Noah?" Cole asked, feeling vulnerable at his sudden need to see a snapshot.

She nodded slowly. Pulling her phone out of her pocket, she scrolled to her pictures. "Here," she said, placing the device in his palm. "I can email any you like."

Noah appeared to be a normal, happy, rambunctious little boy in every picture. His tumbled hair was coal-black. The kid's lively green eyes grabbed Cole's soul and refused to let it go. He looked just like Cole had at the same age.

He had a son who was everything a man could want in a child.

In one shot, Noah raced exuberantly toward a swing set with two other boys about his same size. The untied shoelaces of his sneakers flying, he was clearly ahead.

Competitive, Cole thought, remembering his days as a star quarterback in high school.

"Does he know how to tie his shoes?" he asked.

"Yes. But not all that well because too many of his shoes have had other types of fasteners."

"Then we'll have to work on that," Cole said.

In another shot, Noah was on the yellow roof of a red playhouse with a smiling blonde girl who was missing a front tooth. His goofy grin and wide-eyed look of adoration tugged at Cole's heart.

"Somebody's got a crush," he whispered.

"Her name's Missy. And you're right. I couldn't believe it

when he told me he brushed a spider off of her. He hates spiders with such a passion I knew she was special."

In another, Noah hung upside down from a tree limb like an impishly grinning bat while an admiring Missy smiled up at him.

"Aren't you afraid he'll break something?" Cole asked.

"Oh, yes. He already has."

She took the phone from him and flipped through the pictures until she found the one she was looking for. Then she handed it back to him.

The picture was of Noah lying on a hospital bed. There were dark circles under his worried green eyes as he studied his suspended arm in its white cast.

"What happened?"

"He broke his arm at school while racing a kid down a hill on the playground. Not that a broken arm slowed him down. Within a day he'd learned to do everything one-handed. The only time he complained of pain was when the doctor twisted his arm before he set it. Oh, and he did wax philosophical when he was snuggling with me in bed one morning about how easy it was to break an arm."

"He sleeps with you?"

"No. But he comes in a lot of mornings to cuddle before my alarm goes off."

His son was tough. But he was affectionate, too. Pride swelled inside Cole, and so did another, less easily defined but fiercely possessive and all-consuming emotion.

His gaze locked on Maddie's face. She was the mother of his son. Was that why he felt a profound need to claim her?

"I've gotta go," she said.

"It's a nice day for a swim."

She shook her head. "There's Miss Jennie to see about. She *is* the reason I'm here."

"Well, you call me if you change your mind. Since we

never went skinny-dipping, I say it's time you earned your bad reputation."

"You're incorrigible," she whispered with a grin, lowering her lashes as if she hoped that would lessen the sexual charge of their nearness.

"Call me if you want to swim," he repeated. He touched her arm, running his knuckles down the smooth skin, which caused her to shiver.

"You come over here and try to bully me into a marriage. Then you have the gall to invite me to go skinny-dipping? Neither is going to happen!"

Ten

What was happening to her? What mysterious power did Cole have over her?

Maddie felt both wet and hot beneath Cole's devouring gaze as she slowly peeled her jeans and panties down the length of her legs.

Sunlight poured through the thick canopy of leaves that surrounded them. The blaze lit up the soft scarlet blanket Cole had carelessly tossed onto the grass beside the icy green pool; the blaze lit her up, as well.

How could she so easily succumb to whatever wanton suggestion he tossed at her? How could she do this when Noah's future hung in the balance? Had she no will of her own? Was he right about their marriage being the best thing for Noah? He was certainly right about her wanting him.

Quickly, Cole yanked off his own clothes and laid them on top of hers on a limestone rock. When he gathered her body in his arms, the exquisite shiver that went through her made her cling to him. His warm, rough hands slid down her shoulders and closed around her waist. Then he pulled her slowly down on the blanket and covered her with his powerful body so that his heat enveloped her.

Cole's hands stroked her gently until she was so hungry for him she lifted her legs and urged him to take her. Her whole body was tense and aching for release, but he made her wait, made her beg in throaty, pleading purrs while he stroked and kissed her. Finally, when she felt as though she might explode, he smiled as he slid his body lower down her length so that he could bury his face against her sex. She cried out in pleasure when his tongue caressed and then dipped inside those secret lips.

"Take me," she whispered. "Just take me."

"Patience, my love," he murmured.

Using his seeking mouth and velvet tongue as instruments of pleasure, he soon had her melting and yielding everything. Instead of feeling ravaged and abused, as she had for so many years, she felt cherished and adored.

"You are beautiful," he whispered. "The most beautiful woman I've ever known. You smell good, too."

She felt beautiful, vibrant and aglow.

With a slow, delicate rhythm he licked her, skimming across her velvety interior until she was a quivering mass of nerves ready to fly apart at the slightest flick of his tongue. Only when the pleasure was unbearable, only when she was burning up and on the brink of release, did he stop.

"Don't!"

"Don't what?" he murmured.

"Don't stop."

"Who's stopping?"

Easing his body over hers, he thrust deeply inside her. Arching to meet that one forceful stroke, she came, crying out his name as a sudden gust of wind made the leaves above them swirl in an emerald-green blaze.

"Mine," he growled fiercely. "You are mine."

He crushed her to him even more tightly. Then driven by his own feverish urgency, he began to move inside her, faster and faster, and with such force that he stole her breath. Strange how after his sweetness, she didn't mind his violence and passion. His breathing grew harsh and ragged, and he whispered wildly erotic things in her ear as he carried her to another explosion that was wild and glorious and satisfying on a soul-deep level.

Afterward, when he stared down at her, his green eyes were sensual and tender. Tears pricked against her lashes. How could she feel so safe in Cole's arms?

He ran light fingertips over her breasts, causing her nipples to peak again. Sated with sensual bliss, she smiled up at him as she snuggled closer.

This isn't reality, she told herself. *I can't seriously consider marrying him, especially since his proposal was only about sex and a desire to claim Noah legally. Austin, my job, Noah—they are my reality.* Even if Cole were offering her the life she'd once dreamed of, experience had taught her she couldn't count on him. Greg was steady...and real. He would be there for her. There was no disparity of wealth and social class dividing them. Cole was only a fantasy.

Still, it was nice to be steamy hot and erotically satisfied in Cole's hard arms as a warm summer breeze brushed her body. It was nice running her hands through his hair while she stared past a haze of greenery at the brilliant cobalt-blue sky. She hadn't felt this pleasantly sexy in years, and she probably never would again. But she knew all too well that sex could be a destructive force.

Later, she discovered he'd hidden her clothes and wouldn't let her dress until she went skinny-dipping with him.

"I'm determined to make you live up to your scandalous reputation," he teased.

As they swam in that crystal clear pool, the years seemed to fall away, as did the walls that had protected her heart. During the brief interlude when they splashed and cavorted in the stream, she felt young and carefree and completely happy— as she never had as a girl.

Years ago, some ancestral Coleman had nailed rungs onto the thick trunk of one of the tallest cypress trees. When Cole began to climb, her heart leaped into her throat.

Even though she begged him to come back down, he let out a war whoop and jumped, terrifying her until he hit the water and she knew he was safe. Laughing, he swam toward her from the deeper end to where she stood, her breasts floating above the surface of the water. Reaching for her, he stroked the curving sides of her breasts. The loverlike way he touched them and looked at them, as if he'd never seen anything so alluring, made her feel desirable beyond words.

She wished she could freeze time, but moments like this were as fleeting as the fragile bubbles that frothed below the dam. Smiling, she ran her hands down his body and circled his erection, which she eagerly guided into her own fluid interior, which was warmer and somehow wetter than the water.

She gasped when he circled her with his arms and pressed himself even more deeply inside her. They clung to each other tightly as he began to stroke in and out, faster and faster, until soon she felt she was glowing and pulsating with that all-too-familiar piercing yearning for release.

When she could breathe again, he kissed her brow and held her close. Not speaking, they floated side by side, staring up at the sun-bright clouds through the branches. Later, when they dressed, they walked to their favorite Indian mound and spent half an hour searching for arrowheads. Not that they found much more than a few broken bits of flint. Still, she enjoyed placing her finds in his palm so she could watch while he examined each one thoughtfully.

"Sassy gets here this afternoon," she said as they sat together in his truck in Miss Jennie's drive. "So this is goodbye, because I'll be going back to Austin as soon as I pack."

"Why didn't you tell me earlier?"

"Maybe because I was afraid you'd start pressuring me again."

He folded her slim hand in his much larger one. Turning it over, he brought her fingertips to his lips. "Will you tell Greg about us?"

She hesitated. "I need more time."

"When I want something, I'm not a patient man." He leaned across the seat and kissed her, hard. "Juan keeps calling me and texting me. I've got to leave for the rig in a few hours. If things go as I expect, I can pry myself loose in a week and drive to Austin."

"Not a good idea."

"No—you want to put this off forever." He kissed the tip of her nose and the corners of her eyes and then drew her close against his body. "The quicker we resolve Noah's future and ours, the better."

Reaching across the cab, she brushed her fingertips along his jawline. "I can't marry you."

"That's an unacceptable answer."

A brisk knock sounded on his trailer door. Cole, who'd made no forward progress with Maddie since she'd left Yella a few days ago, had a headache from hell. Clamping his mobile phone against his ear, he stood and strode to the door.

The minute he pushed it open the incessant roar of his rig and its petroleum odors slammed him.

Juan handed him the latest printout and signaled that he needed to talk to him, too.

"Two minutes," Cole promised as he shut the door. "When are you going to tell Greg about me?" Cole demanded of Maddie.

"The more I think about your proposal, the more I think we're not right for each other. I have a life here that doesn't include you," Maddie whispered. "I don't want anything to do with Yella or the past, and you're a part of all that."

"Noah's my son. I won't have another man playing father to him."

"But I can't do without him. We have our big annual fund-raiser this week. Greg offered to sit with Noah that night. And Noah's looking forward to having the evening with him, too."

Cole gritted his teeth. He wasn't getting anywhere over the phone.

After his long silence, she said, "So, how are things at the well?"

Since he had no interest in discussing work, it took him a minute to regroup. "Slow as hell. But there haven't been any injuries, and it's definitely going to produce."

"That sounds really good."

"We've had a few breakdowns. We've had to order parts—parts that had to be back-ordered. Nothing major, just the usual challenges. I need to bring this well in if I'm going to be able to get up to see you."

"I told you. That's not a good idea. The sooner we forget about what happened in Yella, the better."

"Are you out of your mind?" Forget how great sleeping with her had been? Forget Noah?

He hated not being able to see her and touch her. Hell, he was hard just from talking to her. He needed to hold her and make love to her again—if he was to convince her they had to marry.

"I'm getting another call. I've gotta go," she said.

"Greg?"

When she didn't deny it, a nasty green emotion flared hotly inside him. After she hung up, the drilling site seemed desolate and his trailer dreary. Opening a can of tonic water so fast it spewed fizz all over him, he stomped outside to find Juan.

He was losing her. He had to bring this well in fast. Only then could he go to Austin and convince her they had to marry for Noah's sake.

No, he didn't like that she'd slept with him and then had sneaked downstairs searching for her letters. Nor was he happy about the fact that she would never have told him about Noah if he hadn't beaten her to his office. After that stunt, he wouldn't be normal not to consider that maybe there was some truth in what the folks in Yella thought about her.

If there was, that was all the more reason he had to make an honest woman out of her and claim Noah as his son. And even though he had his own doubts, he was willing to ignore them and go up against his family and anybody else who objected to their marriage.

Cole did not want his son growing up the way Adam had, deeply resenting that he was illegitimate. Whether Maddie admitted it or not, by giving Noah his name, he would assure his son of what Maddie claimed was most precious to her—the kind of respectability and sense of belonging that she'd never had.

The sooner he got to Austin and convinced her he was right, the better.

Eleven

His eyes narrowing on the numbers of each house, Cole tensed as he drove up Maddie's shady street for the second time. Her East Austin neighborhood was working-class but decent. Two little girls wearing helmets, big T-shirts and pigtails rode their bikes on the sidewalk. A couple of boys about Noah's age threw a football back and forth to each other.

At least there were kids for Noah to play with.

Probably Cole should have called before coming, but he'd been too rushed. He wasn't happy about having left Juan in charge of the well again, but seeing Maddie sooner rather than later had taken precedence over his business concerns. Noah's future was at stake.

The two-bedroom houses were a scramble of crumbling fixer-uppers and newly gentrified dwellings. Guilt swamped him as he realized she and Noah had probably struggled to survive in far less pleasant neighborhoods before she'd been able to afford even this. If only he'd taken her calls or read her letters when she'd tried to contact him…but he couldn't change the past. All he could do was the right thing *now,* and he *would* do it.

A silver SUV with heavily tinted windows and an aluminum canoe on the rooftop luggage rack swung in front of him and parked in front of a charming white house with a wide front porch. He read the numbers and realized it was Maddie's house.

Damn, he thought as a tall man with broad shoulders, enviable posture and thick, disheveled blond hair jumped out of the SUV and raced up her sidewalk.

Greg? If so, Cole's timing was lousy.

Cole parked on the opposite side of the street and watched a slender, dark-haired boy throw open the door and grin. Rocking back on his bare feet, Noah eagerly grabbed Greg's hand and tugged him inside.

The sight of his son welcoming another man filled Cole with longing, causing his mood to worsen. Nor did his mood improve as he sat outside for another ten minutes studying her sparkling windowpanes and counting, and then recounting, her roses.

Her bright red porch swing made it easy to imagine her sitting outside while Noah played on a nice afternoon. A white picket fence enclosed the backyard. Obviously, she'd made sure Noah had a safe place to play when she couldn't watch him out front, more evidence of her determination to give her son a better childhood than she'd known.

Impatience began to gnaw at him. What the hell was Greg doing inside Maddie's house for so long?

Just when Cole was about to get out of his truck and stomp up the sidewalk and pound on her door, it opened. Maddie, who wore a tight red T-shirt, white shorts and high, strappy sandals, stepped outside clasping Noah's hand. Greg shut the door and then quickly followed behind them.

Cole willed her to glance his way, but she was concentrating too intently on whatever Noah was saying. When she finally saw Cole, she froze.

A wellspring of desire tinged with anger swept through him. Her gorgeous violet-blue eyes framed by thick inky spikes captivated him. She was so lovely, he ached. Somehow he forced himself to wave casually.

Maddie gripped Noah's hand and all but dragged the poor boy to Greg's SUV.

Greg unlocked the doors and everybody climbed inside. When the SUV lurched away from the curb, Cole shifted into Drive and followed.

His mobile phone pinged almost immediately.

Hell, she'd texted him.

On way to Town Lake. Will call u when we get home. Don't follow!

Since he didn't text when he was behind the wheel, he called her back. When her phone went to voice mail, his only option was to leave a message.

"Sorry I didn't call first." Feeling jealous as hell, he hung up.

What was wrong with him? He felt as out of control as a wildly infatuated teenager.

He should go to a hotel, check in, chill, wait for her call. He should call Juan and check in with a few of his engineers.

Since he wasn't feeling all that rational, he stayed glued to Greg's tail.

The threesome parked near the water. From a distance, Cole watched Greg and Maddie unload the canoe and carry it down to the lake while Noah tagged along happily. To get the life jackets, paddles, thermos and cooler, the three of them trooped back and forth, making several trips. Once or twice Maddie glanced toward Cole and flushed angrily.

While they loaded the canoe, Noah knelt on the limestone

bank and sifted through the rocks, stuffing his pockets until they bulged. As a kid, Cole had been equally fascinated by rocks and had spent hours looking for fossils and arrowheads. In college he'd taken several geology courses, a study that had proved useful when he'd gone into the oil and gas business.

He didn't even know his son, but already the boy reminded him of himself.

There was a wide gravel jogging trail along the water's edge, so Cole followed the canoe on foot as far as he could. They didn't stay out long, maybe because Noah's constant squirming caused the canoe to rock back and forth precariously. Not that Greg seemed the least bit put out when forced to return to shore. No, he was a gem, patiently reloading the canoe and repacking the gear into the vehicle. Once they were safely on land and the canoe was on the roof of his SUV, Greg bought birdseed so Noah could feed pigeons. When Noah spilled the first bag chasing the birds, Greg bought another. Growing bored with the pigeons before he was halfway into the second bag, Noah threw the seed down, causing a mad flutter of wings as the gray flock converged on the bag. Pointing at a playground not too far away, the boy raced to it.

Greg and Maddie gave chase and then sat on a nearby bench so they could watch Noah, who was now climbing the colorful equipment. Noah swung, climbed poles, clambered up rope ladders and slid down the slides. When he fell off a swinging bridge and bumped his head, Greg ran over and picked him up. Long after Noah had dried his tears, he was content to hang on to Greg's broad shoulders and watch the other children play.

Hell. Unable to watch Greg with his son any longer, Cole pivoted and strode back to his truck. Climbing inside, he yanked the door shut and jammed his key into the ignition. Gunning the engine, he roared out of the park and headed toward Sixth Street in search of a bar.

Dealing with Noah in the abstract had been easier than seeing him with Greg and realizing that the kid had had six years to form attachments to other people. Illogically, Cole felt angry at Maddie for not telling him and then angry at himself all over again for not being there for her and Noah when she'd first reached out to him.

Six years. Six damn years he'd missed. Would he ever be able to make up for that? One thing was for sure—he wasn't about to give up the years he had left with his son.

Inside the first shadowy pub he found, he ordered a double scotch on the rocks, which arrived before he remembered the vow he'd made not to drink after he'd pulled himself out of his guilt/funk over Lizzie. Sliding the glass angrily aside, he signaled the waiter and asked him to replace the drink with tonic water and a twist of lime. He knocked that back with abandon even though what he really craved was the kick of the double scotch.

Maddie called him while he was having dinner alone. The hotel restaurant's terrace had a view of Town Lake and the sparkling lights of downtown. If he grew bored with that view, there was a friendly blonde in a red sundress who was also alone, sitting at the table next to his, who kept smiling at him.

"I asked you not to follow me," Maddie said.

"Did you tell him about me?" Cole asked.

"I was going to, but I couldn't think clearly with Noah around and you watching us. Plus, Greg had a bad day at school, and I need him to babysit for me during my fundraiser."

"We need to talk—soon."

"This is a difficult week for me. The fundraiser is important to the shelter's survival."

He worried that she was just making excuses. "After see-

ing Noah with Greg I realize how much I've missed. I don'
want to miss any more. The sooner we get married, the better.'

"Look…"

"What about lunch? Tomorrow?"

"Can't. I'm already booked."

"With Greg?"

"If you must know, yes. I didn't know you and I would re-
connect or that you'd find out about Noah when I made the
date."

"Later, then?"

"I've got a completely full schedule at work tomorrow…
and the fundraiser is tomorrow evening. We're always un-
derstaffed, and Casey, my coworker, has a doctor's appoint-
ment tomorrow."

"I'm not taking no for an answer." He said goodbye.

After he hung up, he wondered what he could do to change
her mind about his proposal.

If Nita Stark was a big talker and temperamental as all get-
out, she was also a huge donor and the keynote speaker at the
fundraiser, so Maddie didn't dare rush their call even though
she needed to get off the phone.

When she finally managed to hang up, it was already ten
minutes past noon. She was thirsty and needed to touch up
her lipstick and her hair before she led the tour that she gave
every two weeks. It was a way to inform the community
about the mission of My Sister's House. After that, she had
to meet Greg. Feeling rushed, she grabbed her purse off its
hook and raced out of her office, her high heels clicking on
the polished tile floor.

Even before she reached the door at the end of the hall
where George, her favorite young volunteer, scanned the
area with fierce, earnest eyes while he stood guard for her,
she heard exuberant laughter erupting from the room tha

was used for tours, church services on Sundays and other meetings.

Strange, she thought. Then George pushed the door open and she saw Cole.

"Okay, everybody, she's here," George announced to the clump of women who were gaily laughing at something Cole had said.

"This is Miss Gray. She's going to conduct your tour today," George said.

Cole clapped.

"Sorry I'm late," Maddie began, feeling flustered as she tapped her lectern with her pen while Cole's amused green gaze drilled into her.

Damn him. She'd told him she didn't have time to talk today.

Usually her tour groups were dominated by staid, upper-middle-class matrons who were considering volunteering. Today the women were more focused on Cole than her.

When Cole gave Maddie another slow, insolent grin, she ignored him and began her talk about the shelter. Because he was such an unnerving presence, Maddie spoke fast, too fast, forgetting entire topics she should have mentioned.

Cole, who must have researched My Sister's House on its webpage, asked lots of questions.

"I always thought that places like this just enable dope addicts and prostitutes," he murmured drily.

Smiling tightly, she gave a quick reply. "Anybody who stays in our shelters must agree to drug testing. We are associated with all the best agencies in the city. They can help our clients get jobs, get clean and get their lives back on track. We are not enablers."

"Good to hear. What percentage of your clients do you save? Surely, it's quite small."

It was infinitesimal; still, it was a start.

"Not nearly as many as we'd like," she was forced to admit. Annoyed, she glanced at her watch. "But since I seem to be running a little late, I can't take any more questions until I finish the tour!"

He laughed.

Furious, she raced through her tour while the women remained distracted by Cole. By the time Maddie had completed her talk, she was breathless with outrage.

Ignoring him, she said goodbye to the ladies before handing them off to George. Then she stormed down the hall to her office. Racing to catch up with her, Cole stepped inside the tiny room before she could slam the door on him.

"I'm at work here. I don't have time to play games," Maddie said.

"Who's playing games?" He pulled a check out of his pocket. "Your talk inspired me to write My Sister's House a sizable check."

When she saw the truly generous amount, she grew so hot under her collar she was sure she'd burst a blood vessel. "You don't care about My Sister's House."

"I care about you. And Noah."

"I'll have you know you can't just buy your way into my office because you want to bully me."

"I beg to differ."

"I think you're contemptible."

"Take the check. I'm sure you, as the director, can't afford to turn down a donation that large," he murmured as he placed the check in her trembling palm and folded her rigid fingers over it finger by finger. "Just as I'm sure you wouldn't want me to inform your board that you wouldn't make time for such a generous donor."

She pressed her lips together and took a deep breath. "I will have my board send you a letter formally thanking you."

"I'm sure you will, but I'd prefer a personal thank-you."

"Okay! Thank you." Straightening his check, she slid it into her top drawer. "You've had your fun. Now, would you please go?"

"No. I intend to meet Greg—and Noah—before I leave town. Greg's due here soon, I believe?" He looked at his watch. "Oh, dear, is he late?"

She kicked her desk, wishing it were him.

Grinning, he sat down to wait.

When he refused to budge no matter how hard she glared at him, she sank down into her own chair in weary defeat. In the tense silence that ensued, time dragged and her green walls felt as if they were pressing in on her.

"Okay," he said in a terse tone several minutes later. "You're short on time, so let's not waste it by sulking. I'm here for one thing—to convince you to agree to marry me."

"This is the twenty-first century. You can't force me into a shotgun marriage six years after the fact."

"We have a son. Giving him my name is valid enough reason for me."

"I don't want to involve him in our messy relationship."

"It wouldn't be like that."

"Really? You expect me to believe that after your caveman tactics today? You think because you're a Coleman and I was born a nobody, you can bulldoze over me? You have zero respect for me or my job."

"I attended a public tour. The website made it clear anybody could attend."

"You know what I mean."

"If you think I'm going to sit on the sidelines and let another man father my son, even if that man is a paragon, you don't know me very well. Noah's mine, and I intend to make sure everybody knows it. I'll fight you—until you agree."

She stared at him. His green eyes were as brilliant and stubborn as Noah's. She studied his black hair with its widow's

peak and couldn't ignore his striking resemblance to her darling, if tenacious, little boy.

Cole was so handsome. Even now when she was at log-
gerheads with him, his virile male presence filled the space
of her tiny office in an overpowering way that made her desire him. If she quit fighting him, could a marriage between
them work? They *did* both want what was best for their son.

Sensing that he'd scored on some level, he reached across
her desk and caught her fingers in his. Even that was enough
to make her sizzle. When she felt her cheeks flush, she tried
to will herself to tear her hand from his, but couldn't. So she
shut her eyes and counted to ten before she reopened them and
met his gaze—and felt the same overwhelming need to hold
on to his hand. She'd been alone so long, fighting for Noah
and herself without much help. It hadn't been easy.

"I was jealous during the tour," she whispered. "Of you
and those women."

"Were you really?"

"Ridiculously so," she admitted in a raw whisper. "And I
hate feeling that way…because that's how I felt a lot of the
time when I was growing up. You had all those girlfriends
from good families chasing you, and I was so low in your
eyes, you didn't know I was alive."

He smiled sheepishly and his hand tightened around hers.

"Sorry," he whispered. "I was a beast today. So much was
at stake I felt I had to come."

At his sincere tone, she looked at him in confusion, every
bit as dazzled by his dark good looks as the five women had
been. Oh—she was hopeless. What did he really feel for her?
"Do you really think our marriage could work long-term?"

"If we both work at it." In his eyes, all she saw was tender-
ness and compassion mixed with a profound, burning need.

"I feel like I've built something solid at My Sister's House,"
she said.

"I was very impressed by your tour."

She snorted. "I was awful, and you were flirting."

"With you."

"I feel that I might be throwing it all away if I married you."

"Nobody's asking you to quit your job."

"I used to have this foolish dream of marrying someone who loved me. When I became a single mother, I knew I would have to be more practical. Greg came along, and because of our similar backgrounds, I thought our relationship could work. But you—you and I live in different worlds. You have this huge, legendary ranch, and you own oil fields. You wouldn't be the least bit interested in me if it weren't for Noah."

"Then why did I drive home to Yella when I heard you'd come home?"

"I hate feeling that I wouldn't contribute to your life in any way other than being Noah's mother. I would be a burden."

He leaned across the desk and whispered against her ear-lobe in his deep, musical baritone, both thrilling her and chilling her. "I want you in my bed. Doesn't that count?"

He lusted after her the way every man in Yella had wanted her mother.

But for how long? she wondered, remembering how easily he'd let her go. How would he see her when he no longer felt that way? It could happen soon, if the people in his life who mattered to him refused to accept her.

"You want Noah, so you'll take me, too?"

"If our situations were reversed, and I had him, would you marry me, to be closer to him?"

She would have married the devil to be with Noah.

He pressed her fingers and stared into her eyes. "So, enough of this. What do you say? Will you marry me?"

Before she could answer, she heard quick, determined foot-steps outside her door and jerked her hand free a second before Greg burst through the door. The unruly lock of blond hair that usually fell across his brow was as unkempt as ever. Smiling bashfully, he handed her a vase of limp yellow roses.

"I'm afraid I left them in my car all morning in the heat." His soft brown eyes held genuine regret.

"Why, thank you, Greg," she said, feeling awkward since Cole was staring holes through her. "There's someone here…."

When Greg turned to Cole, she lifted the roses to her nose in an attempt to conceal her nervousness. "Mr. Coleman is just leaving after making a donation."

She glared at Cole frostily, willing him to leave. Greg held out his hand to Cole. "The mission welcomes all donors, large or small. I'm Greg Martin, Miss Gray's fiancé."

"John…Coleman. Most people call me Cole." They shook hands.

"The oilman I've been reading about, who owns Coleman's Landing, who played a hunch and discovered the Devine Chalk oil play over in Devine County?"

Cole nodded. "The same. More importantly, I'm Noah's father."

Maddie's face flamed with a mixture of guilt and anger even before Greg whirled on her. "Noah's father?"

"He was just going," she said.

"Noah's father?" Greg repeated. "No wonder I had the impression I was interrupting something important."

"We ran into each other last week in Yella," Cole said.

"Now I see why you've been so tense and uncommunicative this week," Greg said, glancing at Maddie.

"I—I meant to tell you," Maddie whispered.

Greg turned to Cole. "Maddie told me you were out of the picture…that you wanted nothing to do with Noah."

"I didn't know about him—until she came to Yella last week and we reconnected."

"Reconnected?" Greg's soft eyes glanced at Cole before

settling on Maddie. "I see," he murmured at last, after reading her face.

She resented Cole for forcing this on her. The last thing she'd ever wanted to do was to stun Greg like this or to hurt him.

"Greg, it's too complicated to explain right now, but if you and I don't leave, we will lose our reservation."

"We're not that late. I think I'd like to hear what Mr. Coleman has to say about this complicated matter."

She placed a hand on Greg's sleeve. "No…."

"Maddie and I parted in a rather unpleasant way," Cole began. "I was unaware she was pregnant. When she called to tell me about Noah a year or so later, I was newly married, so I refused her calls…and her letters. Now that I know about Noah, I want to be part of his life full-time."

"Of course." Greg's hurt, thunderstruck tone intensified her guilt.

"While it may complicate things for the three of us, having his father in his life will be wonderful for Noah," Greg said.

Maddie's mouth went dry. She resented the way both men seemed to be making all the decisions as if her opinion didn't matter.

"So—are you free for lunch?" Greg demanded of Cole.

She shook her head. When Cole said he was, she could have kicked him.

"What do you say I bow out, and you take her instead?" Greg said to Cole. His firm tone held a schoolteacher-like edge that she'd never heard before.

"Greg?" she pleaded. "What are you doing?"

"Sounds to me like you and Cole have a lot to work out," Greg said.

"Let me explain!"

"Don't worry. If you still need me tonight, I'll babysit… like I promised."

Then, just like that, he was gone—seemingly out of her life—and she was alone with Cole, whose green eyes glittered with infuriating triumph.

"I'm glad that's settled. Now, will you agree to marry me?"

Twelve

The French bistro where Greg had made reservations was located in a discreet brick building just off Sixth Street in downtown Austin. The waitstaff was French, the food was fresh and authentic, and the softly lit, informal rooms with their lace curtains and their cut flowers in old French liquor bottles had a sweetly romantic air.

Not that Maddie felt the least bit romantic. What she felt was a burning fury that Cole was so determined to have his way that he didn't care who he crushed to get it.

Since the restaurant was so popular, the small rooms were crowded, even at one-thirty, and the two of them were jammed so tightly into a tiny corner booth that every time she moved her thigh brushed Cole's. Despite her anger, she blushed in response.

Sulkily, she ordered her usual *salade verte* while Cole cheerfully ordered a *croque-monsieur* for himself. When their food came, they ate in silence. Only after she'd finished chewing her last scrap of lettuce did Cole speak.

"What time's your all-important fundraiser?"

"Seven," she said, her voice low, tense and sullen.

"What time does Noah get out of his camp?"

"That's none—"

"What time?" His tone was harsh and deliberately calculated to intimidate her.

"Four. But I'm going to leave him in aftercare until nearly six because I've got a lot of work…"

"I want to meet him—before the fundraiser—so change your plans," Cole said. "You're going to pick him up at four and bring him to the house. I'll be waiting for you there."

"That would mean I'd have to leave the office at three-thirty."

"Then do it."

She met his eyes, intending to argue, but his face appeared to be carved in stone. "I have a meeting with a board member at three," she said.

"I suggest you show him my check. Then tell him there'll be more, a whole lot more, tonight at the fundraiser, but only if you keep me happy."

"I'm not letting you take over—"

"I'm not sure you have a choice," he said smoothly. "I can assure you that if you make me happy, you'll have the most successful fundraiser in My Sister's House's history, which you've indicated is crucial this year. Then you'll be able to keep your position for as long as you wish. But if you continue to fight me, not only will you risk losing your precious job, you could end up in an expensive custody battle that you might not win."

She flinched.

"So, back to this afternoon," he continued pleasantly. "If you're smart, and I think you are, you'll tell your board member I'm demanding another meeting with you after four. If you take off early, I promise you, my generosity will more than make up for those lost two hours in your office."

I mustn't let him do this to me! But for the life of her she couldn't figure out a way to stop him.

"I...I'll never marry you after this," she whispered defiantly.

"That's a battle for another day...or night," he said, smiling. "One I don't intend to lose."

Ignoring the way she tensed, he held up his hand and signaled the waiter for the check.

Thirteen

"Oh, man!" Noah shouted from the backseat of her car.

Filled with dread at the thought of Cole waiting for them at her house, Maddie took her eyes off the silver, tanklike SUV ahead of her to study Noah in her rearview mirror. His black head was lowered as he concentrated fiercely on the game he was playing on her cell phone. Glancing back at the SUV, she turned on the radio so she wouldn't dwell on Cole.

Five minutes later, when she turned onto their street, Noah let out a war whoop. "Cops! Oh, boy!" he shouted. "How come they're at our house? Hey, and there's Tristan!"

Tristan, who had carrot-red hair and Harry Potter glasses, was their new next-door neighbor and Noah's new best friend.

When she jerked the wheel toward the curb, Cole and Tristan, who'd obviously had time to bond, rushed toward them.

"Who's that?" Noah demanded as he eyed Cole suspiciously.

Standing tall beneath the flickering shade and brilliance of her huge oaks, Cole's carved features resembled those of a pagan god, harsh and ruthless but dangerously compelling.

"Just an old friend," she whispered in panic.

His hard eyes on Noah, Cole's large, tanned hands were clenched as he waited for them to get out.

She stared past him to the uniformed officers on her porch with false bravado. "What's going on here?"

"There's been a break-in. According to the police, there have been several in your neighborhood. Whoever did it broke a back window."

Just what she needed, she thought wearily as Cole knelt to Noah's level.

"Maybe when the officers finish, you and your friend Tristan here can help me board up the window," Cole said.

"To keep the bad guys out?" Noah said, beaming up at Cole with immense excitement.

"Yes."

"Cool," Noah said.

"I'm Cole. What's your name?"

"Noah. This is Tristan."

"I already met Tristan. In fact, he and I are planning to play some football later."

"Cool! Can I play, too?"

"You'd better believe it!"

"Cool!"

Introductions over, Noah and Tristan dashed up to the porch to watch the police do their work.

Cole stood up. "Good thing I was here to deal with the cops. You look exhausted. How can I help?"

She felt exhausted, both mentally and physically.

"I have the fundraiser to get through, as you well know," she said. "Not to mention whatever ordeal you intend to put me through tonight. Now on top of all that—a break-in."

"All I want is to marry you and take care of you and our son. That doesn't have to be an ordeal, you know. It could be a mutual pleasure."

She shook her head. "I don't see how."

"Looks like I'll have to show you," he said.

Before she knew what he intended or had time to steel herself not to respond, he pulled her to him and kissed her hard.

As always when in his embrace, she lost the ability to control herself or think coherently. His muscular body was rock-hard and her softer figure melted against him. Her wanton pulse raced while flames lit her nerve endings with a hunger that reduced her to a primal, craven creature.

She knew what he wanted—what she wanted—but she was determined to fight it. She wouldn't let him break her heart as he'd done six years ago.

"Stop," she pleaded, even as her body trembled beneath his onslaught. His caressing fingers on her flesh made her blood run hot. "Not in front of Noah!"

He tensed, and she sensed his reluctance to do as she asked.

"For now," he whispered roughly, letting her go.

Shaken, too aware of Noah watching them, she hugged herself tightly.

For his part, Cole stepped back a few feet, as if removing himself from temptation.

Hell, Cole was stunned by how much fun he'd had tossing the football to his son and Tristan while Maddie dealt with the cops. He'd enjoyed helping the kids nail a board over her window, as well, while a flock of grackles fought noisy battles in the highest limbs of her oak trees.

How long had he spent hanging out with the boys while Maddie got ready for the fundraiser—a mere hour and twenty minutes? And already paternal pride swelled inside him. He'd liked Maddie watching them from the windows; he'd liked making himself useful to her while enjoying the boys. Even in this brief time he'd had with his son and the mother of his son, he was surer than ever that he wanted to be a permanent part of their lives, all the time, not just for weekends and holidays.

Noah, who was as bright as a new copper penny, was quirky and cute. He'd shown Cole the Shining Star medal he'd won at school and had liked it when Cole had teasingly started calling him Shining Star.

The boy had a good arm. He could catch passes, too, and run like the wind. Funny how in such a short time, Cole already felt like his father.

He had to find a way to make Maddie see they could be a family.

The fundraiser was under way in the ballroom of one of Austin's fanciest hotels overlooking Town Lake. Shifting masses of elegantly dressed people danced, drank and chattered as Maddie seized the opportunity to slip outside while Cole was surrounded by board members.

Maddie wanted to stay furious at him forever for the high-handed way he'd treated her ever since he'd stormed into Austin. In one afternoon, he had rid her of Greg and made significant advances toward winning his son's affections. Tonight, with her on his arm, he'd easily worked the crowd, seducing most of the shelter's board members and important donors with smiles and witty remarks.

Maybe she hadn't sold as many tickets this year, but Cole had dazzled everybody who mattered when he'd produced a second check that was more than enough to pay the shelter's expenses for a year...and ensure her job.

Leaning against the railing, she stared at the shimmering reflections in the dark lake. He was outmaneuvering her by making himself useful. He'd helped straighten her house; he'd

called her alarm company and arranged for them to rewire
the window as soon as she had the glass replaced.

The music stopped. When Cole's voice came from behind
her, she shivered.

"There you are," he said. "I've been looking for you everywhere."

"It's the first minute I've had to myself all day."

The music in the ballroom started again.

"Dance with me," he whispered against her ear.

When his arm slid around her waist, her heart began to
beat to the seductive pulse of the music. Then he swept her
around and around in a series of expertly executed turns. As
they whirled, the brilliantly lit buildings of downtown Austin
flashed by. Soon, she was breathless and feeling lightheart-
edly reckless.

He made her feel young and almost happy. She'd never
gone to prom or done much dancing. She wanted the music
to go on forever, to dance with him always.

Was he good at everything? Oh, why did it have to feel so
treacherously wonderful to be in his arms?

"You look fabulous," he murmured even as his hot eyes
scorched her skin.

His gaze admired her body in her tight red dress before he
snugged her closer. Then the hard feel of his muscular body
rocked her senses.

"Don't hold me so close," she whispered as she fought a
losing battle against physical arousal.

"I want you," he murmured, ravaging the softness of her
mouth. "Just as you want me. Why did you wear a dress that
skims your body like a second skin if you didn't want to
tempt me?"

She flushed guiltily. When she'd selected the dress tonight,
she'd known she should have chosen something less revealing, but yes, she'd wanted to entice him.

At some point, they stopped dancing. When he lowered his mouth to devour hers, she didn't fight because she didn't have the strength. She wanted him, more than she'd ever wanted anything in her life. Within dizzying seconds, he had her weak and clinging breathlessly.

"We're going home, baby," he said.

"The fundraiser isn't over. I'm still on duty."

"I'll make your excuses," he said in that supremely confident male way that could so annoy her when she wasn't melting with desire.

Five minutes later, he'd made their excuses and they had exited the ballroom. Arms linked, he rushed her to his truck, which he drove with one hand while his other closed over hers with a fierce urgency that had her blood tingling.

Only when they were standing beneath the glare of her porch light did she come back to her senses.

"Good night," she said without unlocking her door. "And thank you—for the check." When he didn't kiss her goodnight and go, she said, "I can't ask you to come in. Greg's here, and Noah…wouldn't understand."

"No way am I letting you and Noah stay here alone after that break-in. I can sleep on the couch."

"No!"

Then Greg opened the front door, and Cole stepped past her into the living room.

"Noah's awake," Greg said. "He had a dream about some witches in his closet, so I've been reading to him."

"I'll take over from here," Cole said.

"No," she began, but she was talking to his back. He was already striding down the hall.

Too tired to fight him, she thanked Greg. After he left, she went to the closet and pulled out a set of sheets and towels and two pillows and tossed them onto the couch.

Determined not to surrender to Cole, at least not tonight,

she went to Noah and kissed his brow, promising that her kisses were magic and would keep the witches away.

Feeling too flustered to look at Cole, she crossed the hall to her own room and closed herself inside.

"One more story! Please! Please!"

"Good night, Shining Star," Cole said as he closed their third book. "Sleep tight." He leaned down and kissed Noah gently on the top of his head.

"If I close my eyes, would you stay here and guard the closet?"

"There aren't any witches in that closet. Remember how we just checked."

"The green one's not there all the time. Just sometimes," Noah stated matter-of-factly. "She looks sort of like an ugly, mean frog. She has snaky hair and big orange eyes. She comes up through a little hole in the floor. Then she grows bigger and bigger, while I grow smaller and smaller. When she's crazy huge, she sneaks out...." Noah broke off, but his enormous eyes remained fixed on his closet.

"It was just a dream. Try not to think about her, okay?"

Cole lay down beside his son and put his arm around him. Shining Star's black lashes lowered heavily to his tanned cheeks. It was amazing how calm and peaceful he looked when he was sleepy.

"Do you think my mommy's pretty?" Noah whispered drowsily.

"Yes," Cole admitted. "I do."

But Noah didn't hear him because he had succumbed to sleep.

Intending to stay with Noah for only a few minutes, Cole loosened his tie and the top button of his shirt. But the bed was soft and Noah was warm and cuddly. Within seconds, he was asleep, too.

Fourteen

In her own room, Maddie unzipped her sparkly red dress and stepped out of it. Naked, she stood in the moonlight, a strange restlessness consuming her. Burning for Cole despite her better judgment, she willed him to come to her. Even as her heart thundered, the house remained silent. Finally, she grew tired of standing all by herself in the silvery light and lay down.

Cole was everything she shouldn't want. He was part of the miserable past she wanted to forget. He was arrogant and determined to force her to agree to his terms. How could a marriage to such a man succeed once their physical attraction died?

Slowly, her eyelids fluttered and she drifted uneasily to sleep. At some point she began to dream.

She was a little girl again, riding horses, happy she could roam far from the trailer and her mother. The trees were emerald-green, the sky a vivid blue. But no matter how glorious her ride, eventually she had to go home, and when she did, the faceless monster was there, barring the door when she entered, grabbing her wrists when she tried to run. She knew that if she didn't get away, he would do the same horrible things to her he'd done before, so she clawed and kicked, but as always he bore her to the ground, and she began to scream.

Her own ear-splitting cries dragged her unhappily to consciousness. When she opened her eyes, moonlight and shadow played tricks on her imagination, causing her to sense a presence in her house even before she heard heavy footsteps in the hall.

Vernon? Was he here?

A mind-numbing fear gripped her. Scrambling across her bed toward the window, she searched for the lock while screaming for all she was worth.

Cole leaped to his feet at Maddie's first piercing scream and was sprinting down the dark hall before her second. When he opened her door, she threw herself behind her bed, where she crouched in the moonlight.

"Vernon?"

Cole's heart shredded. "No! It's just me—Cole."

"Cole?" Her dull, glazed eyes stared at him uncomprehendingly.

"I was with Noah, asleep down the hall," he said. "You're safe. There's nothing to be afraid of."

"You don't know him. You don't know what he's capable of!"

As Cole crossed the room and sank down beside her, he was afraid he did. A terrible understanding took hold even before he pulled her shaking body into his arms. Had that bastard raped her?

"There, there," he murmured.

"Hold me!" she whispered, her intake of breath sharp as she clutched handfuls of his shirt to draw him closer.

"Hey, hey, everything's okay." But it wasn't. Not if his worst fears were correct. He wasn't blameless if what he feared had happened. Far from it.

"No..."

He brushed her hair out of her face. "You've had a bad dream. That's all." He continued to murmur to her soothingly even as he cradled her in his arms, stroking her face and neck while his own conscience attacked him.

Instead of being so hell-bent on protecting his own reputation, he should have protected her.

"Just hold me, please," she breathed, sensing none of his inner conflict. She hung on to him with a desperation that made him ache for what she must have suffered at Vernon's hands.

Why hadn't he seen that he should have done more to protect her? Why hadn't the town seen that she was young and vulnerable and living in a dangerous situation? Suddenly he hated Yella, hated every individual who lived there who'd played a part in this, himself most of all. They'd sat in judgment of her and thus had left her defenseless. She'd hardly been more than a child.

"When...I heard you, I thought Vernon was really here. My dream was so real...I could almost smell him." She began to shudder uncontrollably.

Cole caressed the nape of her neck. "He's in prison, right?"

"Huntsville," she murmured thankfully.

"So, it's okay. You're safe. You're with me. I swear I won't let him or anybody else hurt you ever again."

"You promise?"

"Promise." And he meant it. With every fiber of his being, he meant it. If only she'd give him a second chance, he wouldn't let her down again.

His brow grazed hers affectionately. Then he pressed his nose to her nose, but somehow when he did it, their lips clumsily touched. His blood flamed. And because he felt so guilty, he hated the lust that drove him. But when he tried to pull away, she clutched him even closer.

She was so damn sexy with her huge eyes, her voluptuous breasts crushed against his chest. He inhaled the mingled scents of her shampoo and perfume and grew even harder. She was so soft and feminine, so ripe. When he felt her nipples tighten against his chest, he caught his breath.

It would be easy to slide her nightgown up and strip off his slacks, easy to take her when she was so open to him like this. But he hated himself too much for what he'd let happen, for what he'd willingly ignored. He didn't deserve her trust or her love. He had to process what had happened and deal with his guilt. Somehow he had to get it all straight in his mind.

But when he would have withdrawn his mouth from hers, she clung, kissing him desperately.

"Stay with me?" she begged in such a seductive tone that his whole body jerked with fresh need.

"Not tonight," he said hoarsely.

"Please…."

"Not after your nightmare about Vernon."

Not after he'd bullied her all day, not when she was scared and vulnerable. "You go back to sleep," he murmured gently. "I'll be right down the hall—if you need me."

Even as his heart pounded, he forced himself to push her away and stand up.

"Cole?" Her quick, sharp breaths sounded truly panicked at the thought of being alone.

"I'll be on the couch," he rasped.

Unable to sleep without Cole holding her close, Maddie counted sheep. Then she counted her rushing heartbeats.

When she still couldn't sleep, she got up, paced awhile and then went to the bathroom where she filled a glass with water. Not that any of it helped still her clamoring senses. More restless than ever, she lay back down in the dark.

She remembered Cole's flushed cheeks, the heavy glint of desire in his eyes. He'd wanted her, too; she was sure of it. But he'd been conflicted.

Curious, and feeling shamelessly needy, she arose and padded down the hall to her living room where she found him sprawled on the couch, his dark eyes wide and glued to the ceiling.

"Can't sleep?" she teased.

"Out!" he growled huskily.

"Don't make me beg."

"Can't a guy ever say no?"

Bending over him, she slid her hands under his shirt, feathering her fingertips through the crisp, dark curls that covered the broad expanse of his chest. At his quick gasp of excitement, she seized her advantage, tracing her hands blindly down the muscular length of him, kneading him until she worked her way to the huge bulge of denim between his muscular thighs.

"I thought so," she murmured, closing her fingers over him and stroking purposefully. "I want you naked," she growled into his ear.

He groaned savagely in protest. "Maddie!"

"I want you," she whispered. "But not here." She waited a beat. "My room." She shot him a flirtatious wink and then bolted, flying down the hall, only to be terrified when he did not follow her immediately. She needn't have worried. Two seconds later, they were naked on her bed with her door locked. He had her flat on her back underneath him while he kissed her lips with hot, urgent passion that tore her soul. In an equal frenzy, she kissed him back.

"We've got to slow it down," he whispered.

"No! I need you! Everything you have to give me! Quick. Fast. Hard. I don't want to wait. I need it. I want to erase all the ugliness." She had to erase Vernon for good.

"Then we're at cross-purposes."

With softer kisses and featherlight touches, he slowed the pace and changed the mood. With each tender kiss that he placed on her mouth, on her throat, on each of her nipples and in the center of that damp nest of dark curls between her legs, he made love to her with a reverence she'd never imagined possible.

"Next time I'll protect you," he promised.

"I know."

She wanted him to take her so she could feel his strength and possessive power in every cell of her being, to know that she was safe in his arms. But he lingered over her, loving her slowly, which caused her passion to build to a frenzy.

He placed his lips between her thighs and caressed her with his tongue until her whole body felt on fire.

"My turn," she teased when he would have taken her, "to torture you with my lips and tongue."

She took him into her mouth, sucking gently, teasing him at first and then adoring him. In the blaze of his building rapture, the last vestiges of her nightmare were consumed. There was only Cole and the exquisite, mind-numbing delight she found in his arms.

Suddenly there was a ferocity in them both as he tore free of her mouth and pulled her underneath him and slid inside her.

"Yes," she whispered. "Yes!"

He thrust and she arched, their bodies moving in perfect accord as the world tipped like a crazy top and spun faster. Then they tensed as passion washed over them.

After the explosion, she lay in his arms and wondered if two people like them, from such different worlds, had a chance together.

She awoke to a rosy dawn and noisy grackles, to Cole's hard arms wrapping her with a fierce possessiveness. She felt new and different and yet unable to trust her emotions.

"You look like a little girl when you sleep—a little girl who's every bit as innocent as Noah."

"Not Yella's wanton, wicked bad girl?"

"Don't ever call yourself that again," he muttered fiercely, pulling her closer. "You're the mother of my child. You're going to be my wife."

"Oh, really? What's got you so cocky this morning?"

"How quickly we forget," he said.

"I don't remember accepting any of your arrogant proposals."

"Do you remember the great sex?"

"And that gave you all sorts of ideas about our relationship?"

"If the sex didn't put you in the mood to accept my proposal, maybe I'll have to give you a repeat performance."

"That would be lovely, under different circumstances, but I've got work."

"It's early yet."

"Noah's going to wake up any minute. I don't want to have to explain you."

Instead of arguing, he got up and strode into the bathroom while she lay back and admired his muscular body. After he turned on the shower, he stuck his dark, sleep-tousled head out the door and shot her a grin. "Water's warm. Feels good. I could use some company."

"I really shouldn't. I'm tender as all get-out."

"And we took it so slowly…"

"But we did it so many times."

"We did, didn't we? No wonder I woke up in such a cocky mood. What if I promise to be gentle?"

When she joined him, she kissed him so fiercely he grabbed her hands and held them over her head. Pushing her back against the slick, wet tile he took her hard and fast as the steaming water blasted her. When it was over, she clung to him breathlessly, thinking herself a worse wanton than her mother.

The man didn't love her. He probably never would. And still she wanted him.

Stepping out of the shower, he left her to ponder all the reasons he was wrong for her.

While she dressed, he scrambled eggs and made coffee for them in her kitchen.

"I'm impressed. I didn't know you could cook," she said when she entered the kitchen.

"It's called survival. I can do eggs. I can do toast, bacon, burgers, steaks. I'm afraid that's about it."

She laughed.

After they finished eating, she cleared the plates. "I can't believe Noah's sleeping this late. What did you do to wear him out?"

"Worrying about that witch in his closet wore him out." He paused. "About your nightmare—"

She whitened. "I don't want to talk about it."

"I know." His hand closed over her wrist. "But I need you to sit down and tell me all about Vernon." Something dark in his voice made her suspect he'd already guessed the worst.

The last thing she wanted was to mar the beauty of their first shared morning together by reliving what Vernon had done to her.

"I've got to go to work," she pleaded. "Lots of threads are

hanging loose after the fundraiser. I still have checks in my purse, including yours."

"Sit down, Maddie."

At his fierce expression, she slowly sank back into her chair.

"What did he do to you? I want the truth, the whole truth, and if you don't tell me, I'll find your mother and so help me, I'll force it out of her. If that doesn't work I'll go to Huntsville..."

"No."

"Then why don't you make it easy for me?" He paused. "I don't believe you ever intended to leave me for him. He hurt you, didn't he? You weren't ever in love with him. You left because he hurt you? And because I wasn't there for you when you tried to call me?"

Barely able to breathe because of the fist clamped around her heart, she looked away.

He leaned closer. "Tell me, damn it. Did he do what I think?"

When hot tears of shame leaked out of her eyes, she brushed at them frantically. "I told myself I'd never cry because of him again."

"Just tell me!"

"My mother didn't believe me, so why should you?"

"Did that bastard rape you?"

A desperate sob rose in her throat. She wanted to deny it. If only she could reclaim her innocence somehow, but he saw; he knew.

"My mother said it was all my fault."

"The hell it was."

"I—I tried to stop him. I really did."

"I know, sweetheart. I believe you," he whispered, his voice as agonized as hers. "Go on...."

"But he was so strong. Even though I had a black eye and

a cut lip, my mother refused to believe me. She said I seduced him to be mean to her. When she threw me out, I didn't know who to turn to or where to go, so I called you…and got your mother, who told me how cheap I was."

He shuddered. After an endless pause, he managed, "And then you went to Miss Jennie?"

"Yes. She was wonderful."

"Thank God." He reached across the table and took her hand, pressing her slim fingers hard. "I should have guessed the truth."

"How could you?"

"I don't know, but I shouldn't have been so wrapped up in my own damn ego and pain, so furious and hurt that you could leave me for Vernon that I didn't question your mother or the gossip. I drove you away. I was as bad as everybody else in Yella—worse, because I should have known better since I really knew you."

"I felt so ashamed…"

"I'm the one who should be ashamed. It's a good thing he's locked up, or I'd have to find him and make him pay."

"No." She began to shake. "Then they'd lock you in a cage, too. I don't want that." She paused. "When Noah was around one, Vernon came to Austin. He told me that if I ever went to the police and told them the truth, he'd kill me. You see, he was on parole at the time. He said any infraction could put him away for good. He put his hands around my neck and squeezed so tightly I couldn't breathe…just for a few seconds, just to give me a taste of what it would be like to die, he said. He said Noah would be raised by foster mothers who'd be worse than my mother. After that, I was scared of everything, of my own shadow. Even after he went back to prison for raping another girl, I was still scared. That's when the nightmares started."

"If only you'd called me."

"I did," she reminded him. "You hung up on me because you'd just married Lizzie."

"Oh, God. My sorry treatment of you…"

"It doesn't matter."

"The hell it doesn't! It will always matter. In my own way was worse than Vernon. If I'd claimed you as my girlfriend from the beginning, maybe he would have been afraid to touch you because of the high-and-mighty Coleman name. Did I ever go to your home once? Take an interest in what you had to deal with there? Warn him to leave you alone or he'd have to deal with me? No, I left you powerless, defenseless. *Oh, it matters*. It damn sure matters."

She looked into his eyes and saw everything she needed to see. He believed her.

"You were in college."

"I was old enough to know better," he said, his low tone filled with self-loathing.

"I blamed myself, too. My mother said I'd been asking for it for weeks, dressing sexily to put her down and make her feel old…but I'd only been trying to be pretty for you. I should have been more aware of how I affected Vernon."

"It wasn't your fault. Get that through your head."

"It wasn't yours either," she said, rising from her chair because she wanted to touch him and to be held.

Slowly she slid her hands across his broad chest and laid her head against his shoulder. When his lips brushed her forehead and he pulled her even closer, happiness filled her. His dark head bent over hers. Then he lifted her chin and kissed her gently on the lips. Wrapping her arms around his neck, she inhaled his scent and savored the muscular texture of his body.

She was sighing when the door behind them banged, and Noah hurled himself into the kitchen.

"Can I have pancakes for break—" When he saw his

mother wrapped in Cole's arms, his eyes widened and his bottom lip stuck out.

Stunned, she sprang free of Cole and rushed to her son. Kneeling beside him, she said, "Darling. Mommy's late for work, so we need to get you dressed and ready for school."

Noah stared at Cole. "What's he still doing here? Why was he kissing you?"

"I said we have to get you dressed and ready for—"

"How come you let him sleep over and you never let Greg?"

"Honey, Greg and I broke up yesterday."

"Because of him?" Noah waited. Then he tore free of her and crossed his arms over his thin chest.

"We'll…we'll have to talk about all this later."

"I don't want to talk about it. I don't want to go to school." Noah turned and marched huffily back to his room.

"Do you want me to try to talk to him?" Cole asked.

She shook her head. "I'm afraid everything's happened too fast. I should have prepared him. I think you'd better go," she whispered. "He and I need some time, just the two of us, to work this out. I'll call you."

"No. We've got to tell him who I am—now."

"Not this morning!"

"The sooner we tell him the less confused he'll be."

"You never stop."

"Not when I know what has to be done." He turned and walked down the hall after Noah.

"Cole—no!" By the time she caught him, he was already inside Noah's room.

"I know how you feel," he was saying to their son, "because this is all happening so fast."

"I—I don't understand," Noah said sulkily.

"I'm here because I'm your father. I know it's a shock because I just learned that fact myself."

When Noah's huge eyes glanced at her for confirmation, she nodded.

"I want to take care of you and your mother. I want to marry your mother. I want us to be a family."

When Noah stared at him, Maddie wondered what was going on in his head.

"You could have waited," she said when Cole came back out of Noah's room.

"No. I couldn't. I've already lost six years, and so has he. I want to go to bed with you every night knowing he's in the house and to wake up beside you every morning like we did today."

At the memory of how sweet he'd been last night and this morning, she let out a long sigh. In spite of his pushing so hard, a part of her wanted those things, too.

"So, I've made a little progress?"

"Maybe a little," she admitted.

"Good." Cole pulled her into his arms and gave her a quick kiss. "Go see Noah in case he's more upset than he seemed," he whispered. "I'll see myself out."

Noah, however, was dressed and ready for school. He'd taken the news in stride and was willing to talk to Cole when he called later that night. And because he was, her own objections and doubts lessened.

Maybe Cole was right. Maybe their marriage could work.

Fifteen

One long week later, Cole checked his watch as he rushed up Maddie's sidewalk. He'd made it. It was 5:30 on the dot. He'd even managed to buy her a long-stemmed yellow rose from a homeless vendor on a busy street corner.

As soon as he'd completed his well, Cole had jumped in his truck and driven straight back to Austin.

Not that he was sure he'd find Maddie home yet. The traffic had been so bad on the south side of the city, it seemed very likely she'd be stuck somewhere. But before he was half way up her sidewalk, her front door opened and she ran toward him.

God, she was beautiful in her sexy blue sundress. When he swept her into his arms, her brilliant smile warmed him as nothing else could. He caught the sweet fragrance of gardenias before he crushed her close.

"My well came in."

"Congratulations!"

"How'd your week go?" he murmured, handing her the rose that was a little worse for wear due to the Texas heat.

Taking the golden blossom, she clung to him. "I missed you," she admitted huskily. "Craving you is beginning to feel like an addiction."

He sighed. "I'm just as hooked as you are."

Even though they'd spoken over the phone, being away from her hadn't been easy. She'd tentatively accepted his proposal, and they were trying to figure out how to share their lives. For some reason she was determined that he shouldn't cut himself off from everybody in Yella because of her, and she'd offered to come back to Yella to face both the gossips and her demons.

"You've been through enough there," he'd said.

"We need to give your community a chance to accept me now," she'd said bravely.

"I don't care whether they do or not."

"But I do—not only for your sake, but for Noah's. Your mother lives in Yella. It would be nice if Noah had at least one grandmother."

Because of Maddie's insistence, Cole had already told friends and family the truth about their relationship and the truth about Noah's paternity. They had understood his being infatuated with her in the past and getting her pregnant, but they didn't approve of him being seriously involved with her again. Everybody except Adam warned him to stay away from her.

Not wanting to think about other people's prejudices, Cole pushed a long strand of black hair back from Maddie's face. "Where's Noah?"

"At Tristan's. Watching a movie. Which means we have a little time alone. He'll be home soon, but then they're doing a sleepover, which I planned so we could enjoy—"

"Our own sleepover," Cole finished.

"Exactly." Blue flames lit her violet eyes as he nipped her bottom lip seductively. When he kissed her harder, he felt her body heat against his. He loved how responsive she was.

"Here. I've got something special for you," he said, pulling a little black velvet box from his shirt pocket. Feeling embarrassed, he sank to one knee. "I'm afraid I should have thought of a more original and romantic way to propose."

Taking the box and opening it, she laughed, gasping with awed pleasure when she saw the huge diamond. "Wow!"

"So, will you marry me?" he whispered, looking up at her.

She knelt to his level, her fingertips skimming his cheek. "Yes. *Yes!*"

He took her hand and slid his ring onto her finger.

When she turned her hand to admire it, the diamond flashed. "I definitely can't wear this to work. I'd blind everybody. Or get my finger cut off walking across the parking lot."

"Well, wear it whenever you feel like it."

"Like when I come back to Yella."

"I've been thinking that maybe people there need a little more time to adjust to the idea of you and me."

"So, you've told them about us and they warned you away."

He was silent.

She studied his grave expression. "Have they said things to make you ashamed of me?"

"No. I just don't like giving them the chance to hurt you again."

"I need to go back and face the past, for myself as much as for us. I've been running from shadows for far too long. I gave one incident too much power over me. Since I told you about Vernon, I haven't had another nightmare. It's like this huge emotional weight just lifted off me. I don't understand it. For the first time in years I feel free. And good about myself. I think that if I faced other demons, I might feel even better."

"I'm so glad."

"Maybe I need to convince myself you'll really stand up for me, as well. So, I've made arrangements to get off work and come to Yella for a week or two. I guess we'll find out if we both have the guts to take this thing to the next level. Only you have to promise me that if it turns out one of us doesn't think it'll work, you'll let me go."

He wasn't about to do that. "What about Noah?"

"You'll always be his father. No matter what, I want you to play an active role in his life. It's just that we might not marry..."

"I can't go there."

"What if we both realize marriage isn't the best solution?"

"I refuse to believe that."

It was nearly noon, and Maddie's brow was wrinkled from so much paperwork. She was looking forward to taking a break before her lunch meeting when her phone buzzed. Hoping it was Cole phoning to say he'd arrived safely back in Yella, she blushed as memories of the wild sex they'd indulged in the night before bombarded her. He'd possessed her in every possible way, in every possible position—on her bed, on the floor, against her wall. On her bedroom desk. And she'd reveled in it like the wanton she was reputed to be.

"Hello," she whispered a little too huskily.

"I have a lady in the waiting area to see you, Miss Gray," Lucy, her secretary, said.

"Oh."

"I can't place her, and she refuses to give her name. She looks important."

Maddie smoothed her hair and glanced at her watch. Maddie understood wealthy donors. So much for taking a quick break.

"Show her in."

Seconds later, Hester Coleman, her black silk suit as severe as her face, stood before Maddie's desk. Gloved hands knotted, Hester stared down the length of her long, aquiline nose, her gaze sweeping both Maddie and her tiny office with its stacks of papers and folders on the floor.

In her rush to stand, Maddie knocked over the bud vase with Cole's single yellow rose in it, spilling water onto the stack of envelopes she'd just sealed for mailing.

"Oh, dear." Quickly she set the vase and the rose upright and lifted dripping envelopes out of a puddle of water. Mopping at her desk with one of the paper towels she kept nearby, she attempted a smile.

"May I sit down?" Hester said.

"Why…of course." Nodding nervously in the direction of the chair opposite her desk, Maddie sank back down in her own.

"I know about the child you're using to blackmail Cole."

Maddie went hot with indignation. "I would never use Noah in such a way!"

"How effective to tell Cole now…when he's free again. How else could a girl like you get him to consider marrying you? You don't care what you cost him, do you?"

Maddie did care. "Does Cole know you're here?"

"That's hardly the point. He may be a fool, but I'm not. I'm here to offer you a generous settlement, in cash, if you refuse to marry him."

With her rage and hurt simmering just beneath the surface, Maddie stood up. "This interview is over. I want you to leave my office."

"What? You can't throw *me* out!" Outraged, Hester arose. "When you've cut him off from everybody he's known and loved his entire life, how long do you think you'll continue to fascinate him? He'll resent you," Hester cried. "Eventually he'll leave you."

"Maybe." Maddie picked up her purse. "But you're risking as much as I am. You have a grandson. Do you want to lose him? Do you want to be cut out of his life forever? Is that what you really want?"

Color flamed in Hester's cheeks. "No, but whatever sorrows I might be experiencing as a grandmother, my real distress has to do with my son for becoming involved with a woman who will ruin his life. If you were any kind of mother, you would understand."

Maddie, who hadn't been able to eat more than a couple of saltine crackers after Hester left, had felt so weak and shaken she'd barely been able to function for the rest of the afternoon. Her anger and sense of injustice ate at her. Indeed, she was so upset she made a mess of every project she touched. Finally, she grew so frustrated with herself for letting the woman's words get to her, she went home early.

Once home, she took her phone off the hook and tortured herself by replaying the older woman's vicious looks and cruel slights in her mind. Was Hester right about Maddie's background making her unfit to be Cole's wife? Would their marriage cut him off from everybody he knew and loved? He had said he thought they should live in Austin, so the past wouldn't cloud their future. But she knew what Coleman's Landing meant to him.

After a miserable hour spent beating up on herself for no crime other than having been born who she was, she dragged herself out of the depths and reconnected her telephone. When Cole called five minutes later to ask about her day, she didn't mention Hester's visit. Instead, she gave him the dates for her upcoming visit to Yella.

"Maybe we should put that off and just enjoy each other for a while."

She sensed his hesitation and doubt. He'd been sweet and

understanding when she'd told him about Vernon. But would he fight for her? Did he truly believe in her?

Or did he just want Noah?

Sixteen

Cole looked up from his desk just as his mother's Lincoln pulled up to Coleman's Landing in a cloud of dust. He got up slowly and strode outside to greet her, letting the screen door bang behind him. She'd been on a tear ever since Maddie and Noah had moved in with Miss Jennie for Maddie's visit. When his mother frowned, he knew he was in for it.

"It's hot. I could do with an iced soda," she said coolly when he met her at the door holding a cup of coffee.

He led her inside and brought a soda to the den where she waited for him. "Why did you drive over here when you could have called more easily?" he asked.

"Because I can't stand the way you flaunt your relationship with Jesse Ray's girl so publicly, Cole."

"Maddie's my fiancée, Mother."

"I'm sick of everybody telling me where they've seen her and that gaudy ring you gave her. Sick of the way people are laughing behind your back."

"You've got a lot of influence on the women in this town. Tell them you won't listen to another bad thing about Maddie, and a lot of them will shut up."

Cole hated the way his mother and the people in the town acted toward Maddie, lifting their noses and staring at her coldly, even when she was on his arm and Noah was with them. It was as if they were more against her than ever—just because he planned to marry her. He'd had words with nearly everybody in town. "Maddie is an educated woman who spends her life trying to help the less fortunate."

"I have no doubt about her ability to relate to such people. After all, she's an inferior herself."

"Adam likes her."

"Because he's jealous of you and wants to bring you down to his level. He sees that by marrying her, you'll do just that." Her eyes narrowed. "Besides, Adam's a man."

"What's that supposed to mean?"

"It means he probably finds her attractive…in that base sort of way men find women like her attractive. If you don't watch them, they'll end up in bed together."

Bright, hot anger flared inside him. "I respect her more than I respect the people who are gossiping about her—and that includes you!"

"Because she's using sex and that child to hook you. She'll use the same appeal on Adam and on every other man she meets. Did you know he drops by Miss Jennie's nearly every afternoon to see her?"

"He's doing that to show his support for me." But Cole's gut clenched as he remembered how Maddie had slept with him and then sneaked downstairs to get her letters. How far could he really trust her? Trust either of them?

"Be careful what you say about her, Mother." His doubts made his voice harsh.

"I saw Adam's truck at Miss Jennie's when I drove over

here." She arose. "Enough. I've done my duty. Don't come running to me when you find her in some other man's bed."

"If that's all, I've got work."

He hated himself when he didn't go back to the stack of papers on his desk after she stormed out his front door. Instead, he drove straight to Miss Jennie's, where the sight of Adam's truck parked out front made him go hot with fury. Instead of knocking on the front door, he stomped around to the back where he found Maddie, her face rapt as she stared up at Adam. Not caring that Bessie Mueller was probably watching, Maddie leaned forward to catch whatever Adam was telling her.

"Maddie! Adam!" Cole called.

As the pair sprang apart, Bessie's window shade fell.

Maddie smiled guilelessly as she ran toward Cole. "Adam's been playing football with Noah," she said.

"Noah sure can pass a mean football," Adam said. "But hey, I've got to get back to work—so I can rest from all the running outside in the heat. Your kid's fast." With an easy grin, he tipped his Stetson and strode past Cole.

Maddie watched him until he vanished behind the house. "Your brother's so nice."

Tension made a muscle tick in Cole's jaw. "I hear he comes by nearly every day."

"Noah looks forward to his visits. At least he's on our side and trying to show people he supports us."

Cole was careful to keep his voice neutral. "I'm not sure that's how the town sees it."

"What do you mean?"

"Never mind. Where is Noah?"

"Inside. Playing a computer game." She paused. "What's the matter? Did something happen?"

"My mother came over to tell me people are talking about you and Adam."

Her expression darkened. "And she made you doubt me. So you came over here because...because you thought maybe I was as bad as they say I am?"

"No!"

Her brows knitted. "You still don't trust me, do you?"

"I didn't like hearing about you spending time with somebody else, even my brother. He and I haven't had the easiest relationship. He resents being the bastard son, so that makes him resent *me* at times."

"You don't trust him either?"

"No, that's not what I'm saying." Then why was it suddenly so hard to meet her gaze as she studied him?

"Cole, let's get something clear. I enjoy your brother's company...as a friend. He's the only person besides Miss Jennie and a few of her elderly friends who've been at all supportive of me while I've been here. Several men have dropped by but...they—"

"They hit on you?" She didn't deny it. "Damn it. Tell me who they are, so I can deal with them." He let out a low curse. "For the life of me I can't see why it is so all-fired important to you to stay here and expose yourself to more unjustified criticism by a bunch of dirty-minded gossips."

"Maybe you're right. Maybe I was wrong to come back here. As a kid, I had a fantasy. I used to hope that if people here saw that you cared about me, well, they'd finally accept me."

"When are you going to figure out they don't matter? You're kind and hardworking. You've accomplished a lot. All that matters is that you and I are trying to make a life together for the sake of Noah. We can live in Austin."

"I know. And we will. But Coleman's Landing is your ranch. I want you to be able to come here whenever you like or need to and enjoy it without worrying about me. I want you to be able to bring Noah here, and for Noah to feel safe and accepted."

"The ranch is just a place." He wrapped his arms around her and kissed her hard. She turned into him and clung with a desperation that drove out his doubts, at least temporarily.

"All my life I've wanted to be accepted and loved. Even here. I'm just so afraid that the past and these people will find a way to make you regret marrying me."

"That's not going to happen. I'm not going to let it happen. When are you ever going to learn that other people's opinions don't matter all that much?"

"That's easy for you to say, since you've always enjoyed their good opinions."

Holding her close made his breath quicken. She'd been baring her soul, and suddenly all he wanted was her naked. He needed to make love to her so he could focus on what mattered instead of the town's vicious lies about her. "Hey," he murmured, "I was wondering if you think we could sneak off for a swim? Just the two of us?"

Her sparkling gaze lifted teasingly to his. "I'd have to ask Miss Jennie to watch Noah."

"Do it."

"Can we please get chocolate pudding for our picnic with Cole?" Noah asked as Maddie pushed their grocery cart down the aisle past a row of boxes of instant pudding.

"Pudding is not on Cole's list."

Noah scowled as he struggled to read a label on a box.

"However...he did put down chocolate chip cookies."

"But can we have pudding, too? Please, can we?" Noah's bright green eyes pleaded.

"Okay," she said, smiling. "One. Just pick one."

"Oh, boy!" Noah leaned closer to the puddings so he could concentrate on the words and pictures.

Maddie caught a whiff of all-too-familiar whiskey breath and looked up in alarm.

"Is that your brat?"

The woman who'd spoken was shuffling clumsily toward them. When she burst into rough laughter, Maddie felt an icy chill race down her spine. Kneeling, Maddie clutched Noah closer.

Caught off balance, he dropped a box of pudding and sent it sliding down the aisle straight at the woman.

"Hey, my pudding!" he cried and would have run after it if Maddie hadn't held him fast.

"You're a bad child!" the woman scolded. "Just like your mother was."

"Pick another pudding," Maddie ordered through clenched teeth even as she stood up and whirled her cart around to escape.

But the woman, who was faster, lurched toward Maddie and seized her cart. "You think you're too good to speak to your own mother, do you? Because that fool Coleman gave you a big rock and says he's marryin' you? Well, you're not, girlie. You're no different than me. You should hear what people around here are saying about you. They say you snuck around…chasing him when you were a girl 'cause he was rich. They say you lucked out…havin' 'is baby, keeping it a secret, so as you could make him pay for it later. If they play, make them pay. That's what I taught you, baby girl, didn't I?"

Maddie was desperate to get Noah away from this woman, who was kin to her biologically but in no other way. Several shoppers, who had frozen to watch their embarrassing exchange, were standing together in a tight little clump, their mouths hanging open. No doubt they'd heard every ugly word and believed every ugly lie and would repeat them to anyone who would listen.

Feeling the weight of their contemptuous gazes, Maddie's

mouth went dry. But it was her mother she most wanted to escape. Feeling queasy, it was all she could do not to abandon her grocery cart, grab Noah and race out of the store.

But she wouldn't cower or give any of them the satisfaction of seeing how devastated she was, so, instead, she notched her chin higher and drew herself up straighter. Shoulders back, she marched toward the checkout counter where she waited patiently while Noah tugged at her jeans, begging for candy while the teenage checker with multiple piercings took forever to scan their groceries.

Seventeen

Tears streaming down his cheeks, Noah burst into Miss Jennie's kitchen like a tornado.

"Don't stomp or run in the house," Maddie said to Noah as Cole, who was drinking coffee at the table, looked up from an agricultural journal.

"I hate Bobby Mueller! I hate him!"

"Remember now, we don't hate people. We may get angry at them," she said. "We may not like what they do, but we don't hate them. And what did I tell you about slamming doors?" Noah's chest rose and fell with impotent fury as he struggled to process what must have seemed like very ill-founded advice.

Cole's dark brows drew together. "What's wrong, son?"

"Mueller called me bad names." Warily Noah approached the table where they sat. Then his face contorted with misery as he stared up at his mother. "He called you a bad name, too, Mommy. He's always calling you bad names. Then Luke and him laughed. They say you're a bad lady because I don't have a daddy."

"That's bull," Cole thundered. "Why didn't you tell them I'm your father?"

"Easy," Maddie murmured.

"Easy? No way! You want me to go easy on the morons in this town who attack you?" His carved face fierce, Cole turned to Noah. "Listen to me. The next time you see that big-mouthed brat, you tell him who I am."

"But you're not married to Mommy!"

"Okay, you're right. I should have married her a long time ago. Before you were born. But do you see that ring on her finger? It's called an engagement ring. I gave it to your mother because I love you and because I'm going to marry her. Soon. But we don't have to be married for you to know you have a daddy."

"Really?" Noah asked, his eyes brightening ever so slightly. "Can I tell Mueller?"

Cole and Maddie both spoke at once.

"No," she said very firmly. "Stay away from him."

"Yes," Cole said. "Tell him if he says any more bad things about your mother, you're going to tell me, and I'll go over there. Then he'll have to deal with me."

"Will you beat him up? Oh, boy! Can I tell him right now?" Noah demanded eagerly.

Maddie felt her collar tighten. "I don't think…"

"Sure," Cole said, meeting her gaze. "Why not? If you don't fight for what's important to you, you don't have a chance in hell of getting it."

Noah leaped for the door and raced out of the house, banging the screen behind him even harder than before.

Maddie turned on Cole, but he spoke first. "I think we've given everybody in this town long enough to get used to the idea that we're getting married. And where has it gotten us? Brats are attacking Noah. I say we move on to the next step."

"But they don't accept us as a couple."

"Who says they ever will? I know their acceptance is important to you, but I say to hell with them. What matters is being a family for Noah."

How did he feel? she wondered. He wanted Noah, and he liked to sleep with her. But what kind of person did he believe her to be? Could he ever feel close enough to her to share his soul, to love her? Would she always feel this guarded and defensive around him because she wasn't sure he thought she was good enough for him?

"Let's have our engagement party," he said. "We'll invite everybody you're so set on impressing out to the ranch for the best barbecue in the county. I'll hire the best band. They can come or not—whatever. We'll get married a week later and move to Austin. Then they can gossip all they want to."

When she would have protested, he arose and pulled her into his arms. "I'm tired of sleeping at the ranch and you and Noah sleeping here. Every night just seems to get longer and lonelier."

At his words, Maddie felt something hot and wanton flicker to life inside her.

"Don't make me wait any longer," he demanded, his low, hoarse tone holding more impatience than ever.

"All right," she finally agreed. "All right." Not that she felt completely sure of him. Still, she repeated, "All right."

The ranch house exploded with music and people, people who were making it obvious they didn't want her in Cole's life.

Maddie needed to get a grip, to relax, so that she could at least pretend to enjoy herself at her engagement party. Not easy, since she was in an overly sensitive mood that had her feeling everything was false, even the few smiles tossed her way. She could think only about one thing: Would Cole have considered marrying her if Noah hadn't been in the picture?

If only he respected her as much as he lusted after her. If only he'd let her wear something she'd picked out instead of the sexy blue number that shimmered and clung to her body like a second skin.

"I want them to eat their hearts out because you are so beautiful," he'd said.

Apparently curiosity trumped disapproval in Yella, Texas, because nearly everybody who'd been invited had come. Or else, like most Texans, they were all addicted to barbecue.

Exhausted from having worked so hard to put a party together on such short notice and from standing in three-inch heels in the receiving line for nearly an hour, she roamed the throng jamming the rooms of Cole's brilliantly lit ranch house. Her stomach growled, reminding her she hadn't eaten in a while, but she felt too nervous to eat spicy barbecue. She considered going outside where a tent had been set up and a second band played, but decided that maybe she needed a drink to settle her nerves first.

Four young women she'd gone to high school with brushed past her on their way to the bar without even looking at her while several men she'd known her entire life stared at her with lewd frankness. When she glared back at one of them, he smirked. The only friendly faces belonged to Cole's employees.

Halfway to the bar she saw Hester, so Maddie ducked into a shadowy corner to search for Cole. Finally she found him in the middle of a group, talking to Becky Weber, a beautiful brunette who'd been Lizzie's best friend. Just as Maddie was about to move out of the shadows and go after her drink, leaving Cole to his conversation, a deep, friendly voice behind her said, "There you are. I've been looking everywhere for you."

She whirled. "Adam!"

"Would you care for a drink?"

"I'd love one."

"What would you like?"

"Pinot grigio."

He vanished, returning with it almost immediately.

"That's some dress," he said, his friendly brown eyes skimming her figure. "You look stunning."

She blushed self-consciously. "Cole bought it for me and wanted me to wear it." She smiled. "I'm so glad you showed up. At least now there's one friendly face."

"Wouldn't have missed it. I know what it's like to have Hester Coleman against you. Cole doesn't. His mother's relentless. In her opinion, I'm the bastard brother who doesn't belong, and you're the wrong girl for Cole. She thinks she's protecting Cole and the family, but in truth, she's so insecure she's easily threatened and excessively territorial. Bottom line, we've both got to fight to win any sort of acceptance here. I've made a little headway, but it's slow going."

When his dark face began to spin against the sea of people, she realized she shouldn't have drunk the wine before she ate.

"I should be used to it," she said with a pretense of bravery, but her voice quavered a little. "I shouldn't care so much about her opinion at this point in my life. Mainly, I just want to know how Cole truly feels about me."

"He's marrying you, isn't he? He plans to move for your sake, doesn't he? Since I grew up without seeing much of my father, I can speak from experience. His marrying you will be good for Noah."

"I know."

"You feel like getting some air...or maybe dancing?" he asked.

Since Cole was still engaged with Becky, she nodded. "Maybe the fresh air will clear my head." Smiling, she took his arm.

* * *

The whole time Cole had been surrounded by Becky and several of Lizzie's dearest friends, he'd been aware of Maddie, who looked vulnerable standing all alone in her dark corner. Before the party, he had imagined her triumphant, dazzling everyone in her blue dress. She was being very brave, but he could tell she was struggling to hold her own.

Thus, at first, he was grateful when his handsome brother brought her a drink. Then his friend Lyle, who'd been watching Maddie the whole night, jabbed Cole and shot him a lewd smile.

"Knowing who she is and what she's capable of, I'd be afraid to leave her alone for long…even with my brother. They look pretty chummy, don't they?"

"Would you lay off?" But Cole couldn't help glaring at the pair.

"If they're that friendly in public, what do you suppose they'd do behind your back? I hear he's been dropping by Miss Jennie's a lot lately."

"To play ball with my kid."

"Right." Lyle chuckled.

Cole watched Maddie incline her head toward Adam, saw Adam lean down to catch what she was saying, saw him smile as he put his big, tanned hand under her arm to lead her out of the room.

Why the hell was Adam taking her outside? Surely they weren't leaving together? What about Maddie? Didn't she know she was making a spectacle of herself?

Suddenly doubt had white-hot jealousy boiling to the surface. Clenching his hands, he fought for control.

He trusted Adam. And Maddie…

Then he saw his mother eyeing him triumphantly.

Misreading Cole's silence as tacit agreement with his insulting comment, Lyle elaborated. "Nobody says you and your brother shouldn't enjoy her, Cole. We just don't think either of you should marry her."

Suddenly Cole's fist shot into Lyle's smug jaw with such force he sent the man stumbling backward onto the hardwood floor where he lay spread-eagled, staring up at the ceiling as he rubbed his jaw.

"Damn it, Lyle, don't you ever say another word about Maddie! Do you hear me? I'm marrying her, and I don't care what you or anyone else in this room thinks!"

"But what do *you* think about her, Cole?"

Cole started, aghast at his behavior. Lyle had struck a nerve. Yes, he wanted Noah, and he wanted Maddie in his bed. But would he ever feel sure of her?

As his guests watched in shock, Cole leaned down and yanked Lyle to his feet. "Get the hell out of my house!"

Lyle scrambled for the door. When he was safely out of Cole's reach, he said, "Did you see that? He hit me! He's crazy! She's made him crazy! You're a damn fool to marry her, Coleman, and you know it!"

Cole raked a hand through his black hair. "Sorry about the disturbance," he muttered before he plunged out of his house in search of Maddie.

He must have looked upset because when Maddie saw him, she got up from the chair where she'd been sitting beside Adam and ran to him.

"Are you all right?" she cried.

"We're leaving," he said.

"Okay, but since this is our engagement party, are you going to tell me why?"

"Because I just lost it in there."

"He hit me—because I told him the truth about you and Adam. And I told him that he'd be a fool to marry you just so he could sleep with you, and he knows I'm right," Lyle yelled at her as he roared past the porch in his truck before driving away in whorls of dust.

"Is that true?"

Cole flushed darkly.

"Because of me? And Adam?"

"He said something I didn't like."

"And you believed him? You thought that your brother and I...that we were flirting or worse?"

"No, I just didn't like him saying it. I couldn't let him get away with talking about you like that."

"Because you don't trust me."

"I do trust you. It's just that..."

"No, *you don't*. You don't respect me. You're just like they are, ready to believe the worst of me at the slightest provocation—because you believed him, just a little. Or more than just a little."

"No, I got mad. I lost it. I'm not feeling too good about it either."

"You'll always be the high-and-mighty Coleman, and I'll never be anything but Jesse Ray's daughter."

"That's unfair. You're blowing this out of proportion... just like I blew what he said out of proportion."

"Maybe, but there's a grain of truth. For your information, your brother was just being nice to me...*because* everyone else was ignoring me. He was explaining how he understands how I feel, because sometimes he sort of feels like an outcast here, too."

When she looked up, she saw that Cole's mother, and everybody else, was staring at her.

"I've never felt so absolutely cheap and humiliated in my whole life as you made me feel tonight," she whispered. "You believed what Lyle said—instead of having faith in me."

"No! I got jealous!"

"I hate to say it, but your mother was right. She said you were attracted to me solely for the sex."

"That's not true."

"It is. It's all you see in my friendship with your brother—who's a really sweet guy, by the way—who's also having a rough time in this town."

"I know his problems a helluva lot better than you do."

"Sex is not enough to hold a marriage together. So, if you'll be so kind as to lend me your truck, I'll drive myself home to Miss Jennie's. Then I'll pack and return to Austin. Miss Jennie will call when I'm gone so you can pick up your truck."

"Damn it. I'm not letting you go."

"This isn't going to work, Cole! You need a woman you and your friends can respect, a woman you can trust and be proud of."

"You're that woman."

"I wish I was, but I'm not. Not if you found it that easy to believe I could hit on your brother at our engagement party!"

"I got jealous, damn it!"

"Well, I don't want you marrying me because you feel obligated, because we have a son. I want my husband to love and trust me. I grew up without love, so maybe I've wanted that my whole life!" She paused. "Look, I told you—you can see Noah whenever you like. But we can't marry because you don't respect me, and I need your respect more than I need anything else. Added to that, I don't want our marriage to cut you off from everybody you're close to."

"I don't care about them! I want to live in Austin. With you."

"You cared enough to hit Lyle. No matter what you say, you'll come to resent me in time. If I let you go, you'll find someone else, someone who fits in the way Lizzie did, who's really right for you."

"And you'll go back to Austin and settle for Greg?"

"No. Being with you has taught me what it's like to feel passion. You've helped me grow stronger. I'm not going to settle again because now I know I deserve someone who loves me and who respects me, too."

"But I love you and respect you."

"I wish you did, but you don't. You're just saying you do to get your way."

"I was a fool. I made a mistake."

"You're right about one thing. We both nearly made a terrible mistake."

Slowly she slid her engagement ring off her finger and handed it to him. "I'm feeling very tired, Cole. I need to lie down. Will you please give me the keys to your truck so I can go home?"

When he reluctantly dropped the keys in her hand, she walked away, stumbling on the first stair of his porch, maybe because the tears that had been threatening to fall were blinding her.

Cole rushed forward to help her, but she cried out when his fingers grazed her elbow. When she turned, and he saw the raw anguish in her luminous eyes, he realized how profoundly he'd hurt her.

Struggling to push him away as the whole town of Yella gaped, she said, "Don't touch me! I won't allow you to treat me like I'm something low and despised."

"I don't despise you. *I love you!* I swear I do!"

"I don't believe you," she whispered on a heartbroken sob as she hurried past him toward his truck.

Eighteen

Cole felt as though his soul was shattering into a million pieces. He stood in the barn outside Raider's stall listening to the music drifting from the ranch house, where his engagement party remained in full swing.

He loved Maddie, but like a fool he'd never told her until tonight. He'd probably loved her for years.

A pain as terrible as what he'd felt when he'd believed Maddie had left him six years ago fisted around his heart and squeezed hard. Only when she'd run from Yella had he learned how much she'd meant to him—that he couldn't live without her.

For six years, he'd endured, breaking Lizzie's heart in the process. He didn't want to suffer like that for the rest of his life, or make some other unlucky rebound lover suffer as he'd made Lizzie suffer.

How could he have gone on believing that maybe the gossips were right about Maddie? "How did I screw it all up so fast, Raider, old boy? What the hell can I do to get her back?"

The gelding rasped in a breath. Then he snorted.

"I have to get her back."

Raider's ears pricked forward. Then Cole heard a footstep behind him and turned to see Adam striding into the barn.

"You didn't totally kill your engagement party. There's still a few diehards. Your mother just left."

"At least someone's happy."

"I don't think so. Surprisingly she seemed a little chagrined. In fact she asked me to find you. So, do you wanna punch me, too?"

"I think I've made enough of an ass of myself for one night."

"For once, you admit it," Adam said.

"For once, I won't resent you throwing it in my face. Look, I know you had it harder than I did growing up without our dad. But that wasn't my fault!"

Adam smiled. "Who else can I blame? Dad's dead, and you're here. But I want to talk about Maddie. I don't resent you so much that I'd try to come between you two. I was just trying to be your brother and her friend."

"I know. I just let a stupid remark get to me."

"I like Maddie. I like Noah. I think you and she are right for each other."

"Like it matters now. Don't you get it? I crushed her. In public. In front of the idiots she was trying so hard to impress. Worse, I made her feel like she has to apologize for who she is. She left me."

"Good for her. By the way, you look like hell—which means you've probably already figured out how precious she is to you. You're not going to let her go back to Austin, are you?"

"How the hell am I going to stop her?"

"Why don't you go over to Miss Jennie's and throw yourself on her mercy? *Crawl. Grovel.* She's not like the hardhearted gossips who despise her. Unlike them, she's got the softest heart in the universe. You love her. And she loves you. What else really matters?"

Maddie felt like throwing the phone at the wall.

"What? I can't believe you sent him over here! Well, I don't want to talk to him, Adam!" Maddie cried. "I'm packing, so I'm going to hang up!"

"No, you're not! Because I'm your future brother-in-law. And you're not that rude."

Through her tears Maddie stared at the brightly colored T-shirts spilling out of the suitcases on her bed.

"What part of 'I broke it off with him' don't you understand? He'll never respect me! So, no, I don't want to talk to him. If you send him over here, I won't answer the door."

"He looks terrible," Adam said.

"That's not my fault."

"He loves you."

"No, he doesn't. Not if he thinks I'm capable of the same sort of low, despicable tricks my mother's capable of."

"You're wrong. I'm not saying he didn't behave like a fool. Or that he didn't totally embarrass you. He did. He messed up *because* he loves you. Guys only screw up big-time with the women they love. Lyle hit a nerve, and Cole lost it."

"Look, I have to go. I'm throwing things in my suitcases as we speak."

"Now you're being an even bigger fool than he was. You two are good for each other. You know it. Have you ever been this mad at anybody else before? Or felt this hurt?"

"No!"

"See there!"

"You're crazy! I'm hanging up!"

"Don't throw it all away. Relationships always require some give along with the take. He's Noah's father. You grew up without a father just like I did. Do you want to do that to Noah?"

"That last was a low blow."

"He hurt you. Get over it."

No sooner had she hung up the phone than Miss Jennie appeared at the door. "Who was that, dear?"

"Cole's interfering brother. Adam was trying to talk me into forgiving Cole."

"But you're much too angry to even consider that, aren't you?"

"This has nothing to do with anger. It has to do with the fact that Cole will always see me as Jesse Ray's daughter. And I've always tried so hard to be more than that."

"You've always been more than that."

"You see it. You always saw it. But Cole isn't capable of seeing it."

"He is a man with a man's blindness, but I believe he loves you, and that no matter what his failings, he's always loved you. Maybe tonight made him realize who you really are."

"And snakes can fly."

"Horrid thought," Miss Jennie said, causing Maddie to smile. Miss Jennie paused. "You know that I lost my darling Raymond in the Korean War, and I never found anybody else."

"I know."

"Think about that. You could go your whole life and never find anyone you love half as much as you love Cole. Or find a man who loves you as much."

Maddie was silent as she considered the long, lonely years that would stretch ahead. For no reason at all, she thought of the intense way Cole looked at her sometimes.

"Raymond's dead, so I could place him on a pedestal. I can always think of him as absolutely perfect. I've conveniently forgotten all our silly squabbles and his many faults. It's really quite nice to have this perfect fantasy lover who never disappoints you. But life can be so messy. I think all men, however desirable, are the messiest of creatures. They have such limitations. Cole fell back into old habits, old thought patterns. Look at his mother, the woman who raised him. I never told anyone in Yella this, but she and I grew up in the same town. Did you know she grew up poor? That she was abandoned in a Dumpster as a baby by a teenage mother who was sent to prison? That she wasn't adopted by the wealthy family who raised her until she was six years old?"

"No."

"She's very insecure and has worked hard to keep those secrets. No doubt she worked just as hard to try to instill all sorts of extremely silly ideas and prejudices into her son. He got jealous and suffered a momentary lapse of judgment and hurt you, which I'm sure he profoundly regrets."

"But—"

"I'm not finished. Unfortunately, at the party, you fell back into the old pattern of feeling left out. And you reacted defensively by lashing out at Cole. Self-worth comes from the inside, Maddie, and you have plenty of it…most of the time. But we all have our weak moments, and find ourselves filled with self-doubt. That's all that happened. He got jealous at the wrong moment. You weren't your best self either, and you took it out on each other. It was bad timing. Don't throw away something as precious as the love of a lifetime without being sure it's the right thing to do."

"Oh, Miss Jennie, will he always see me as an easy, untrustworthy sort?"

"You won't be the first woman ever to face the challenge of convincing a man how lucky he is to have you. Trust me, if he doesn't know your true worth now, he will."

* * *

Maddie stood in the open doorway of Miss Jennie's house as she anxiously waited for Cole to drive up. After he cut the engine, she took a faltering step across the porch toward him, and then another. He got out of Adam's truck and walked toward her just as slowly, as if he felt as unsure as she did.

"I...was waiting out here for you because Adam called me and told me you would come," she said breathlessly. "I was so hoping you wouldn't change your mind about coming... about me...about us."

"Forgive me," he whispered.

"I was every bit as much at fault as you."

"No, I knew how important it was to you to make a good impression on everybody, and what did I do? I made you wear that sexy dress that you didn't feel comfortable in."

"Because I have hang-ups."

"Because you're you. I'm sorry for what I did. For what I said. I need to respect your feelings. Then that lout insulted you—I should have defended you instead of behaving like a perfect ass."

"I should have been more understanding. But I'd been feeling sort of abandoned and isolated while you talked to Becky, so when you accused me..."

"You felt violated," he said.

"I don't want to rehash everything," she whispered. "It was painful enough the first time around."

"Yes. But there is one more thing. Lyle just called me on my cell, after drinking several cups of coffee, and apologized. He said he was out of line...about everything. He said you were the loveliest woman there in that sexy blue dress, and he was drunk and jealous of me. He said I was lucky you'd have me. He said he was going to call my mother and tell her it was high time she quit bad-mouthing you to everybody in town. He said he was going to call you and apologize."

"That's...that's kind of nice."

"I thought maybe you'd like it."

She smiled. "Yes, but I see now that it's what I think about myself that matters."

"So, what about it—will you still have me?"

She caught her breath and pulled him close. "I love you so much, I'd be crazy not to. I overreacted, too. I was feeling scared at the party surrounded by all those people, imagining them thinking the worst of me. Maybe I was looking for an excuse not to face up to the past and simply let it go. So what if I had a lousy childhood? I'm a success now. You're more important than the past. I love you too much to let you go so easily."

"You sure scared the hell out of me."

"I scared myself, too."

He laughed. "I love you. I've always loved you. I was just too big an idiot to see it."

"I love you more."

"I guess we have the rest of our lives to argue about that."

"You're forgetting something," she whispered.

"What?"

"My engagement ring. I want it back!"

He laughed. Reaching into his pocket, he pulled it out. She held up her hand, and he slid it on. Then his lips found hers, and she forgot about the ring, forgot about everything but how much she loved and wanted him.

He loved her, too. Imagine that.

He'd always loved her.

Epilogue

The ballroom where their glittering reception in Austin was held had sparkling views of Town Lake. Not too many people from Yella had come to celebrate her marriage to Cole, but she didn't care all that much because her dear friends from Austin were there.

Somebody tapped a knife on a crystal glass to silence the throng.

"A toast to the bride," rang Hester Coleman's imperious voice.

"Oh, no," Cole muttered as he took Maddie's hand. "Mother, I don't think—"

Maddie squeezed his fingers. "No, she's been nice to me lately. Maybe she's turning over a new leaf. Let her say whatever she has to say. It's enough that she's here. Whatever she says, I promise you that I'll be okay."

"But this is your day, not hers," he said. "I want it to be perfect for you."

"Life is messy," she said, winking at Miss Jennie when she caught her eye.

"In a long life, people make mistakes," Hester began. "I've made my share. Today, I wish to toast to the happiness of my son and grandson and daughter-in-law. I wish them all joy and long lives!"

"Well, that wasn't too bad," Cole muttered, clutching his bride close. "Maybe she's coming around."

"Maybe," Maddie whispered. "Until she does, we have each other again. That's all that really matters."

Noah went up to Hester, and the older woman's face lit up as she knelt to chat. Maddie thought of her own mother, whom she hadn't invited, whom she wasn't ready to forgive and maybe never would be. At least with Hester there was the hope of a better relationship in the future.

Cole pulled her close and kissed her, not caring if his mother and everybody watched. Her groom's kiss swept her away, and she was only dimly aware of the joyous applause that surrounded them, only dimly aware that his mother was clapping, too.

Then Noah left Hester and ran to them. Leaning down, Cole lifted his son into his arms.

"Are we married now?" Noah asked joyously. "Are you my daddy for real?"

"Yes," Cole said, hugging Maddie to him with his other arm. "For real and forever."

* * * * *

#2239 ZANE

The Westmorelands

Brenda Jackson

No woman walks away from Zane Westmoreland! But when Channing Hastings does just that, the rancher vows to prove to her that there is no man for her but him.

#2240 RUMOR HAS IT

Texas Cattleman's Club: The Missing Mogul

Maureen Child

Hurtful gossip once tore Sheriff Nathan Battle and Amanda Altman apart. But when Amanda comes home, will an unexpected pregnancy drive a new wedge between them or finally heal old wounds?

#2241 THE SANTANA HEIR

Billionaires and Babies

Elizabeth Lane

Grace wants to adopt her late sister's son. Peruvian bachelor Emilio wants his brother's heir...and Grace in his bed. Can this bargaining-chip baby make them a *real* family?

#2242 A BABY BETWEEN FRIENDS

The Good, the Bad and the Texan

Kathie DeNosky

Wary of men but wanting a baby, Summer asks her best friend, rancher and bullfighter Ryder, to help her conceive. But can he share his bed with her without also sharing his heart?

#2243 TEMPTATION ON HIS TERMS

The Hunter Pact

Robyn Grady

Movie producer Dex Hunter needs a nanny, and Shelby Scott is perfect for the role. But when the script switches to romance, Shelby balks at the Hollywood happy ending, at least at first....

#2244 ONE NIGHT WITH THE SHEIKH

Kristi Gold

Recently widowed King Mehdi turns to former flame Maysa Barad for solace. But as forbidden desire resurfaces, betrayal and secrets threaten to destroy their relationship once and for all.

REQUEST YOUR FREE BOOKS!

2 FREE NOVELS PLUS 2 FREE GIFTS!

HARLEQUIN *Desire*

ALWAYS POWERFUL, PASSIONATE AND PROVOCATIVE

YES! Please send me 2 FREE Harlequin Desire® novels and my 2 FREE gifts (gifts are worth about $10). After receiving them, if I don't wish to receive any more books, I can return the shipping statement marked "cancel." If I don't cancel, I will receive 6 brand-new novels every month and be billed just $4.55 per book in the U.S. or $4.99 per book in Canada. That's a savings of at least 13% off the cover price! It's quite a bargain! Shipping and handling is just 50¢ per book in the U.S. and 75¢ per book in Canada.* I understand that accepting the 2 free books and gifts places me under no obligation to buy anything. I can always return a shipment and cancel at any time. Even if I never buy another book, the two free books and gifts are mine to keep forever.

225/326 HDN F4ZC

Name	(PLEASE PRINT)
Address	Apt. #
City	State/Prov. Zip/Postal Code

Signature (if under 18, a parent or guardian must sign)

Mail to the Harlequin® Reader Service:
IN U.S.A.: P.O. Box 1867, Buffalo, NY 14240-1867
IN CANADA: P.O. Box 609, Fort Erie, Ontario L2A 5X3

Want to try two free books from another line?
Call 1-800-873-8635 or visit www.ReaderService.com.

* Terms and prices subject to change without notice. Prices do not include applicable taxes. Sales tax applicable in N.Y. Canadian residents will be charged applicable taxes. Offer not valid in Quebec. This offer is limited to one order per household. Not valid for current subscribers to Harlequin Desire books. All orders subject to credit approval. Credit or debit balances in a customer's account(s) may be offset by any other outstanding balance owed by or to the customer. Please allow 4 to 6 weeks for delivery. Offer available while quantities last.

Your Privacy—The Harlequin® Reader Service is committed to protecting your privacy. Our Privacy Policy is available online at www.ReaderService.com or upon request from the Harlequin Reader Service.

We make a portion of our mailing list available to reputable third parties that offer products we believe may interest you. If you prefer that we not exchange your name with third parties, or if you wish to clarify or modify your communication preferences, please visit us at www.ReaderService.com/consumerchoice or write to us at Harlequin Reader Service Preference Service, P.O. Box 9062, Buffalo, NY 14269. Include your complete name and address.

HD13R

SPECIAL EXCERPT FROM

HARLEQUIN®

Desire

USA TODAY *bestselling author*

Kathie DeNosky presents

A BABY BETWEEN FRIENDS, *part of the series*

THE GOOD, THE BAD AND THE TEXAN.

Available July 2013 from Harlequin® Desire®!

They fell into a comfortable silence while Ryder drove through the star-studded Texas night.

Her best friend was the real deal—honest, intelligent, easygoing and loyal to a fault. And it was only recently that she'd allowed herself to notice how incredibly good-looking he was. That was one reason she'd purposely waited until they were alone in his truck where it was dark so she wouldn't have to meet his gaze.

The time had come to start the conversation that would either help her dream come true—or send her in search of someone else to assist her.

"I've been doing a lot of thinking lately…" she began. "I miss being part of a family."

"I know, darlin'." He reached across the console to cover her hand with his. "But one day you'll find someone and settle down, and then you'll not only be part of his family, you can start one of your own."

"That's not going to happen," she said, shaking her head. "I have absolutely no interest in getting married. These days it's quite common for a woman to choose single motherhood."

"Well, there are a lot of kids who need a good home," he concurred, his tone filled with understanding.

"I'm not talking about adopting," Summer said, "at least not yet. I'd like to experience all aspects of motherhood, if I can, and that includes being pregnant."

"The last I heard, being pregnant is kind of difficult without the benefit of a man being involved," he said with a wry smile.

"Yes, to a certain degree, a man would need to be involved."

"Oh, so you're going to visit a sperm bank?" He didn't sound judgmental and she took that as a positive sign.

"No." She shook her head. "I'd rather know my baby's father."

Ryder looked confused. "Then how do you figure on making this happen if you're unwilling to wait until you meet someone and you don't want to visit a sperm bank?"

Her pulse sped up. "I have a donor in mind."

"Well, I guess if the guy's agreeable that would work," he said thoughtfully. "Anybody I know?"

"Yes." She paused for a moment to shore up her courage. Then, before she lost her nerve, she blurted out, "I want you to be the father of my baby, Ryder."

Will Ryder say yes?

Find out in Kathie DeNosky's new novel

A BABY BETWEEN FRIENDS

Available July 2013 from Harlequin® Desire®!

HDEXP0613